the Blue Mirror

the Blue Mirror

KATHE KOJA

Frances Foster Books

Farrar, Straus and Giroux / New York

Copyright © 2004 by Kathe Koja
All rights reserved
Distributed in Canada by Douglas & McIntyre Ltd.
Printed in the United States of America
Designed by Nancy Goldenberg
First edition, 2004
10 9 8 7 6 5 4 3 2 1

www.fsgkidsbooks.com

Library of Congress Cataloging-in-Publication Data
Koja, Kathe.
    The blue mirror / Kathe Koja.—1st ed.
       p.   cm.
    Summary: Seventeen-year-old loner Maggy Klass, who frequently seeks
refuge from her alcoholic mother's apartment by sitting and drawing in a
local café, becomes involved in a destructive relationship with a charismatic
homeless youth named Cole.
    ISBN 0-374-30849-7
    [1. Emotional problems—Fiction. 2. Artists—Fiction. 3. Homeless
persons—Fiction. 4. Runaways—Fiction. 5. Mothers and daughters—
Fiction. 6. Alcoholism—Fiction.] I. Title.

PZ7.K825 B1 2004
[Fic]—dc21
                                                        2003048510

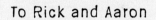

To Rick and Aaron

the Blue Mirror

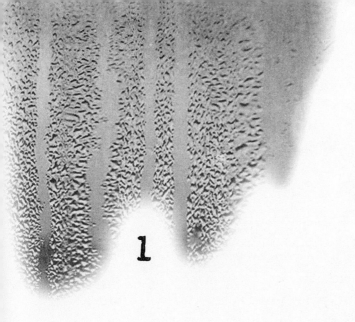

1

This room: square apartment box, cruddy carpet and bent plastic lamp shade, rain down the windows in jagged silver lines. On top of the TV, Paz curls in a ball. And Monica, lumped on the plaid sofa, her slack face in TV light: sugar-frosted hair and a million wrinkles, twenty years of Winstons and vodka. And tears. Once I saw her crying in her sleep.

And me: keys and jacket, scuffed blue messenger bag strapped on like a life preserver, moving quiet in the TV's echoed drone. I fill Paz's bowl, run my hand down his sleeping black back, reach for the door—but then Monica stirs, eyelids crimping: "Maggy? Are you going out?"

Waiting, one hand on the door. If I don't answer, maybe she'll go back to sleep.

"Maggy? Where're you going?"

Where I always go: downtown, to the promenade, the Wishing Well. To the Blue Mirror, where I belong. "I'll be back later," I say.

"Maggy?" Fully vertical now, a coaxing smile, like a little girl who never grew up and never will. "I'm almost out of cigarettes. Run get me some?"

My pause, trying to think which is worse: letting her smoke when she's half asleep, and maybe start a fire; or letting her get antsy until she gets up and goes by herself, maybe lets Paz escape again. Last time he almost got out of the building, one of the neighbors found him wandering by the downstairs door.

Finally "All right," I say. "I'll get them while I'm out, and come back early. All right?"

She's slumping again, slipping down on the cushions like a building imploding. They say vodka has no smell. They're wrong. "OK, that's good, that's good. Thank you, baby," as I close the door, turn the dead bolt; *baby*. In a year and three months I'll be eighteen. Old enough to live on my own, get a job, go to art school . . . Savannah, or Chicago, or College for Creative Studies, I don't know. Casey says the wrong school is worse than no school at all. Not that I can afford to go to school anyway.

Outside, the rain's turned into snow, chilly puddles everywhere, the bus flings back a rooster tail of slush.

Most of the kids at my school have their own cars already; all of them have driver's licenses. Except me. Maggy the Exception.

The bus smells like diesel, wet feet, and damp newspaper. Head against the window, I don't need to pay attention, I know which stop is mine. I've been coming down here since eighth grade, a million years ago. It used to feel like such an adventure: catch the bus—the real bus, not a school bus—and ride it all the way downtown, to the promenade, the big fountain that people call the Wishing Well. Tourists throw change in it, and the homeless kids, the runaways and skwatters, fish it out. If the weather was nice, I'd sit on one of the concrete benches around the fountain and draw. If it was crappy out, like now, I'd go to the library, or the Historical Museum, someplace dry; you can stay in places like that a long time, even a kid alone can. These days I just go to the Blue Mirror, and nurse a grande cappuccino for three hours. And draw.

Now I'm almost there, but first I have to stop: LIQUOR BEER LOTTO, the burned smell of pizza so old it looks like jerky, the fat guy behind the counter gives me a slippery smile. "What can I do for you, honey? Nasty night out there, isn't it?"

"Two packs of Winstons."

He rings them up, then pauses, hand on mine on the money on the counter. "Are you sure you're legal, honey? I'm not supposed to sell tobacco to minors."

"I'm twenty-two," as I pull my hand away, jam the

cigarettes deep in my bag. I can feel him watch me walking out: checking out my ass, the creep, or else he thinks
I'm going to steal something. Or both.

At the Blue Mirror it's really crowded for a weekday
night; the snow, probably. I can't get the booth I want, the
one right under the window, blue-tinted window almost
as big as the wall, showing café and street in equal reflec-
tions, your own face ghosted on the faces outside: the real
blue mirror. *When you're, like, a famous artist,* Casey
says, *I'll make them put up a plaque. The Maggy Klass
Memorial Booth.*

Sure. Famous.

Hey, have a little faith in yourself, will you? I do.

Casey's the only one who's ever seen my sketchbooks,
my own personal paper world: it's called "The Blue Mirror," too. Everything I see as I sit here goes into my
sketchbook, made alive again in a different way, like a
fairy tale I tell myself: tourists, skwatters, bicycle cops,
winos and shoppers and dogs, all translated into giants
and magic bikes and stop signs that talk, princess-girls
with no faces, reptile-boys who steal purses and guzzle
down the coins. Anything can happen in "The Blue Mirror," anything I want.

Casey says it's amazing, the parts I've let him see, anyway. . . . Casey's not working tonight, it's Thursday. But
even without him the Blue Mirror makes me feel good,
camouflaged safe in the steam and chatter, the dark
strong-coffee perfume; if I could bring Paz here I'd never

leave. And—just as I'm turning away from the counter, cappuccino in hand—like a granted wish my booth gets empty, the girls there sliding out: three girls, two princess-types in fluffy white jackets and Yo Chica jeans, gold bracelets loaded with jingly charms, and the third a sort of skwatter-girl, I can't really make her out. She's grimy like a skwatter, hair in greasy, curly strings, but she's dressed kind of like a princess, spike-heeled boots that must have cost a fortune, and she's wearing this blue lipstick that I've never seen before.

Still a trio, they step out to the sidewalk, where the skwatter-girl palms something to the other two, quick and practiced, I can't see what so it's probably pills, tabs of Double-J or something. One of the princesses digs in her teeny-tiny purse, hands the skwatter money, and they separate, two left, one right, but not before I see the jangly gleam, bracelet fresh around the skwatter's wrist, she's smiling blue to herself as she skips away, really skips, like a little kid, across the jostle of the street to the corner opposite—

—where her friends are waiting, one a dumpy little bundle of bandannas and scarves, I can't tell if it's a boy or a girl—but the other one, I look at him once and I can't look away. Like the most perfect picture you ever saw, a walking wish come true: crow-black hair and loose green jacket, tall, even taller than me but when he moves it's not jerky or gawky, just pure grace, like he really belongs in his body, like it's his favorite place to be.

And when he smiles, oh it's sweet and secret both, like spiked candy, his lips that same strange blue, he's laughing as the skwatter-girl shakes her bracelet, the girls laugh, too, and I'm scrabbling for my sketchbook, oh my God I have to get him, I have to catch that smile—

—but I can't, he moves too fast, comet quicksilver off the curb and it's like the traffic parts for him, he just, just *glides* across the street—

—and then a bus, slush and puffing exhaust and when it passes he's gone, they're gone, just the crowd that without them is suddenly empty, just the nightly frieze of passers-by, just me in the blue window with "The Blue Mirror" on my lap . . . so I draw what I can, what's not there but was: three shapes, outlined in little dashes, like beings from some brighter world just skwatting on this planet, passing through to check the natives, too fast and wonderful to ever stop and stay.

I stay, of course, where else am I going to go? I sip my cappuccino, making it last; I sketch the homeless guy on the corner, wrapped in his cloudy plastic cape, a human hill grown out of the concrete and trash; I sketch the way the snow falls, strikes the glass and turns to rain—but it's only busywork, my hands but not my head, the night's work is over now and I know it. So I do what I always do when I'm done, date the page at the bottom and sign it: *mags*, in a tiny circle. *mags* is my secret name, my alias or nom de plume or whatever an artist would call it, like it's me but not-me, the best part of me, the part that draws.

I've never told anyone about it; even Casey doesn't know about *mags*.

On the way back, the bus is always colder. I sit with my knees up almost to my chin, arms wrapped around me but still I'm freezing, hands turtled into my sleeves, wondering, like a bad habit, what I'll see when I get home. Will Monica be sleeping? or yelling back at the TV? or trying to cook herself a midnight meal? Once I came home and found firemen there: she'd tried to make dinner and almost melted a Teflon pan, the whole place was full of toxic smoke. We sat out on the landing, waiting for the stink to clear, and one of the firemen took me aside: *You might want to get some help here, Miss, you know what I mean?* Well sure, but what I want doesn't much matter, does it? Monica doesn't want any help.

But tonight when I turn the lock, burglar-quiet, all I find is her knocked out and snoring, empty glass sticky on the floor, the ashtray tilted full beside her. I move it, shut off the TV, shuck my jacket, and pick up Paz, pink yawn and stretching, almost as glad to see me as I am to see him. We climb under the blankets to lie in the darkness, his steady lawn-mower purr against my chest, as I feel my hands and feet slowly get warm again, eyes closing to find the image, like a favorite page from a picture book: Prince Charming on a street corner, distant and beautiful, smiling again in memory that radiant, blue-lipped smile.

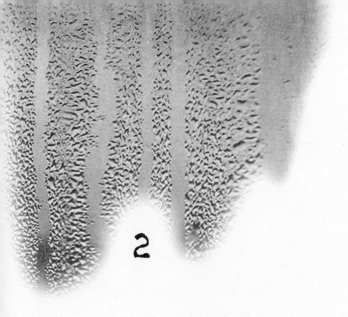

2

People say a lot of things about high school: *It's the happiest time of your life,* or *It's the worst place in the world,* stuff like that. To be honest, the topic doesn't really interest me, but if hanging out at pep rallies and sneaking smokes in the parking lot makes a person happy, then hurray for her, right? And the woe-is-me, end-of-the-world, school-is-ruining-everything stuff—come on, people. Don't act like this is real life.

I didn't always think this way. Back in middle school it all mattered to me, mattered more than anything: I showed up every day, went to all the classes, worried nonstop about my grades. I was going to get a scholarship, a free-ride scholarship, I was going to go to college some-where far away. But now all I want is to keep doing "The Blue Mirror," so civics and pre-calc and language arts, how can any of that help me? It just wastes time. And energy. But if I stayed home every day with Monica I'd go completely crazy, and you can't walk the streets all day, so school's not that bad a place to hang out: it's warm and dry, the computers are new, and they have herbal tea and muffins in the cafeteria.

And the classes are crowded enough that, with a little planning, you can be there and not-there at the same time, or at least there enough that no one's going to make a huge stink about it. Especially with Monica, who'll call in to excuse me when I need her to. So I go mostly when I feel like it, and don't when I don't.

One class I do feel like going to, almost always, is Sculpture I, which I have to take to get Drawing II next semester—but that's OK, I just like being in the art room, the smell of it, chalk and oils and turpenol, that underwater-skylight glow that reminds me a little of the Blue Mirror. I can't do the actual sculpture; no matter how hard I try, all my pieces end up looking like a preschooler's version of Mickey Mouse, but Ms. Onwiski—she's the teacher—says not to worry, the motor skill will come: *You already see what's there, Maggy. You just need to see it in the clay.* Ms. Onwiski's the one who keeps giving me the art school brochures, like if she gives me enough of them I'll finally cave in and go. . . . Casey says I'd like it in Chicago. I wonder if he's ever been there? I wonder if he's ever seen that dark blue smile?

I know it's stupid, but I can't stop thinking about that guy: black hair, pure mercury grace, like someone from "The Blue Mirror" come to life, a dream come true. . . . Will I ever see him again? or have I missed him forever, no more chance to catch him, sketch him, I wonder if Casey might know who he is? I can ask tonight, Casey always works Fridays: *For the tips*, he says, which is a joke, hardly anyone ever tips but he works all the hours he can, he wants to be assistant manager, then manager, then *Who knows? Maybe I'll buy this place, give you all your cappuccinos for free.*

Free is good.

It's hard not to worry about money, especially since I never have enough. Monica doesn't have a job; she used to, when I was a little kid, when my dad was still around. She was a therapist, a PT aide at a nursing home, helping people in and out of wheelchairs, teaching them range-of-motion exercises, stuff like that. But she hurt herself somehow, lifting a patient or something; she was even in a wheelchair herself for a while. Now she gets a disability payment, a check every month. And child support; what a joke. If it was really *child* support, they'd make out the checks to me. . . . I think my dad lives in Iowa; I'm not sure. He used to send Christmas cards but he doesn't anymore. I suppose I'd miss him if I knew him, but all I remember is them fighting, and her crying, so how can I miss that?

Now the bell goes off, a buzzing tone like a giant metal bee; Ms. Onwiski nods at me, *See you.* Outside the parking lots are full, car horns beeping, people waving, yelling plans for the weekend. No one asks me what my plans are. What would I say if they did? My life is so far removed from theirs I might as well be on another planet, I might as well be in "The Blue Mirror" myself, my own character with mirrors for eyes, there beside my charming prince, my kind of prince, in ever-after land. I wish.

As I walk home, it starts to snow, minuscule flakes like glitter, sparkling in the weak white sun. Monica's gone— maybe to the doctor's, or the liquor store, the two errands she can't get me to do—so I decide to clean up a little, straighten the blinds and the sofa pillows, throw out the newspapers, swab down the coffee table gritty with glass rings and ash. This place wouldn't look so bad if someone took care of it, but Monica's pretty much hopeless, and I don't always have time.

Paz watches from the top of the TV; he likes to perch up there, where it's warm. I found Paz downtown, a baby Dumpster-diver, little skwatter kitten smuggled into my room until Monica started thinking we'd always had him. He's amazing-looking: golden eyes, black velvet fur, pure confidence as he follows me to the kitchen, expecting something good—and right away he gets it, a scoop of fresh food in his bowl. If only that was the way the real world worked.

Snow thickening now past the windows, from powder to powdered sugar, deeper still by the time I've finished dinner and Monica slogs in, drab and deflated, her coat off in slow motion, Band-Aids on her arm. She lights a cigarette and looks at me with big sad eyes.

"They gave me shots today."

I don't say anything. She gets shots every month. Paz pads off, to my room probably, to cocoon on my bed. I lace up my boots, off-brand Doc Martens, but they keep out most of the wet.

"You're not going out, are you? In this weather?"

"It's not that bad," and really, it isn't, more snow but no wind so the cold doesn't cut so hard. And the bus is warm and almost jolly, the driver playing muted Motown on her little pocket radio, she smiles at me as I pass and I smile back; another, bigger smile for Casey, who takes his break when I come in: "Tonight's special," as he steps around the counter, two cups in hand. "Have one on me. . . . So what's happening on Cartoon Planet?" tapping my sketchbook. "Any new stuff to show?"

I open to yesterday's page, the lines of motion, the almost-there and "I saw this really cool guy," I say. "Him and his friends, outside. But when I went to draw them, they were gone."

"A cool guy, huh?" He has gray eyes, Casey, soft gray like a pencil smudge, and dishwater-blond hair that goes in all directions; his smile is broad and wide. "New guy? Should I be jealous?" He's just joking, I know, but I feel the blush anyway, my mushroom skin turning measles-red, I *hate* that but " 'S OK," Casey says; he taps my hand, slides out of the booth. "Break his heart, that's fine. Just don't let him make you any coffee."

He goes back behind the counter, I pick up my pencil. *Break his heart*, sure. Like I even know how. I've never had a boyfriend, not really; in freshman year a couple of boys asked me out, I went to a few of the dances, and that was it. Mostly they just wanted to have sex as soon as possible. And whenever I tried to talk to them—about art, or books they might've read, or life outside of school—they just looked at me like I was from Mars; they never got any of my jokes. And I never ever for a second considered showing them "The Blue Mirror," or even the Blue Mirror; why would I let them into a world they couldn't even guess was there?

I see other girls, girls at school or on the street, I watch what they do with guys and it's not so much how? but why? What are they getting out of it? Sex, I guess, and something to do on the weekends. But what about—I don't know—having someone to *be* with? to talk to, to show my drawings, to show myself? Not the shadow me that ghosts through the days, guarded and wary, a gaze under glass, but the real me, the "Blue Mirror" me, both sides of the glass at once. Who is out there, for me? Anyone? Or am I always going to be alone?

The cappuccino warms me, cinnamon and sweet; I open my sketchbook. From my booth the street's a snow globe, people passing in the drift and swirl: the homeless cape-guy, shuffling in place to keep warm; an older couple, laughing, arm in arm; a UPS man rushing by with a late delivery—

—and around the far corner, like a magician's trick, abracadabra here they come: the princess-skwatter, the little bundle, and him. Heads together and laughing, that wide amazing smile, he's got his arms around both of them, steering them, yeah, this way, they're going to pass right by the window, right by me—

—and as they do, I'm ready this time, I look with all my might, I *see*: frayed green jacket, black hair snow-damp, those perfect blue lips, and up this close I can see his eyes are black, too, no brown at all but pure dark, like deep water, deep as a shadow at noon—

—and he's smiling through the window, he's smiling at me

—right at me

—and pivoting, turning around, oh my God they're coming in now, *he's* coming and *bam*, in a panic I shut my book, I sit up straight, I look everywhere but the door but "Hey," beside me, right here beside me now; I can feel the cold coming off him, like the night itself come inside and "See?" he says. "I told you she's an artist. Didn't I tell you?"

I stare at the tabletop, pencil still in hand. My face is

red as a sunburn, baking from the inside out and "Yeah?" says the skwatter-girl, one hand snaking for my sketch-book, charm bracelet dangling bright; her nails are filthy. When I look up, it's her eyes I see, brownish-gold, they remind me for a second of Paz, a mean Paz; her blue mouth is a sneer. "What's that? Your coloring book?"

I put my hand on the cover, holding it safely closed. The little bundle—pudgy cheeks, crooked teeth; now I see it's a girl, younger than me, maybe even middle-school age—she laughs, a breathless, nervous sound, like she isn't sure if that's funny or not.

But "Hey," he says again, even softer, he's leaning down so I have to look up: right into that smile, teeth so white against the blue, such a strange color, more like paint than lipstick. "It's OK, Marianne's just messing with you. . . . Right, Marianne?" squeezing her shoulder as she pulls away, sullen, the way a little kid would. "And this," nudging the bundle, "is Jouly. Say hello, Jouly."

"Hello."

And then he waits, waits for me to ask, I have to know so "What's your name?" I say, but my voice comes out hoarse, trembly and dry like I don't talk much, *calm down* but now his cold hand's pressing mine, just a little, there and gone and "I'm Cole," he says, and slides into the booth beside me, gently pushing my sketchbook aside. Marianne and Jouly sit across, Marianne scowling out the window, Jouly pick-picking at her hands, her chewed-up nails, she's wearing gloves with the fingertips cut out. Why am I even noticing these things, why don't I just look at him? But I can't. He's too—*there*, too real, so all I do is glance, glance away, glance again like touching something hot until "My name," I say, "is Maggy."

"Maggy the artist. You come here to draw, huh?"

Marianne makes a scoffing sound, *yeah right*. "Why don't you go draw the tourists?" she says. "Set up on the sidewalk, maybe they'll throw you some quarters." Jouly laughs, looks at me, stops. Pick-pick-pick.

Cole ignores them both. "So what're you drawing, Maggy?"

You: but of course I can't tell him that so "All kinds of stuff," I say instead, hands tight on the cover, like it might fly open by itself. "Whatever I see."

"What do you see?" in a different tone, sideways to face me now, like we're all alone in the booth, the Blue Mirror, the world, but "I'm *thirsty*," Marianne loud across the table. "I wanna *drink*."

Cole checks his pockets, shrugs at her, looks at me, and "You want a, a coffee or something?" my voice steadier now, digging in my bag though there's not much there, but it's enough to buy three coffees, one for him, one for Jouly who drinks two-handed like a hungry little dog, one for Marianne who doesn't drink at all, just glares out the window as Cole talks to me, not a conversation but a kind of story about the streets, about fooling the transit cops, ducking in doorways to thwart the cold, about the way the Wishing Well looks on a winter day: "Like, like little trapped stars, you know? when it freezes around the edges of the basin, the way the new water hits the ice and kind of sinks, have you ever seen that? It's just, it's fucking beautiful, isn't it?"

Trapped stars, that's it exactly, the fresh drops trembling through the crust. . . . So he can see things, too, see like me, those endless dark eyes but "What time is it?" he says, cup down; he checks the wall clock. "Damn, I gotta go. Will you be here tomorrow?"

Don't go. Don't ever go. "I'm here every day."

"Then I'll see you, Mags—"

—*what?* what did he say? but they're already out of the booth, out the door, down the street walking as three; Marianne hooks her arm around his waist, does that mean that they're together? And Jouly, hanging on his sleeve, what's—

"—with them?" Casey, busing cups from the table, looking past me out the window. "You know that guy, or what?"

"That's Cole," I say. I can feel myself smiling. "He's the one I saw before, the one who—"

"Oh." Brows up, he smiles back at me but not his real smile, he's thinking something but I don't ask, I barely notice because all I can think is *Mags*, how did he *know*? How could he possibly—

"—nice of you. To treat them. Him."

"What?"

"Just don't make a habit of it, you know? People like that—"

"Like what?"

His pause, rearranging the words in his head before "Street kids," he says, carefully. "They have their own agenda, they're not like you. You know?"

Of course I know, I've been watching them, drawing them, for years: all the runaways and pill heads and skwatters, begging and shoplifting, hanging around the Wishing Well, sleeping in the warehouses and the empty storefronts by the river. Every week the Promise House van drives around, rusty-red van with a yellow cross, to give them sandwiches and condoms and buttons that say PROMISE ME. Every winter a bunch of them go away, grow up, go to jail, whatever, and in the spring a whole new crop sprouts up, like the grass between the sidewalk cracks. But some of them stay longer, a lot longer. The homeless cape-guy was probably once a skwatter.

So "I know," I say to Casey, "I know all about skwatters." He looks at me a minute, then shrugs and takes the emptied cups back to the counter as I flip open my sketchbook and get to work, the image like a soap bubble in my mind; my job is to try to hold it long enough to get it on the page, catch it before it pops. So I draw, and draw, I could draw all night, chase them, him, all over the paper: quicksilver and blue, here and gone, like a dream you wake from much too early—

—until I notice how quiet it's gotten, the Blue Mirror emptied out, past eleven already and "Maggy," Casey calling from the storeroom, "hey Maggy, you're gonna miss your bus!" and oh shit he's right so: scrambling for my sketchbook, my coat, the last bus home already chugging at the stop as I sprint, bag smacking my back, "Wait! wait!" to tumble into the seat, out of breath but smiling, I can't seem to stop smiling.

Even Monica notices, slouched on the couch squinting at TV: "You happy, baby?" like it's some rare occurrence, like a solar eclipse. "You have fun tonight with your friends?"

"Sure," as I edge past her, way too up to sleep, stretched on my bed staring into the darkness, Paz a warm ball on my stomach: Happy? Is that what this is?

I'll see you, Mags. Tomorrow.

I'm still smiling.

But outside the Blue Mirror it's Marianne I see, hunched like a troll in Cole's green jacket and "Hey," sharp when she sees me, taking her hands from her pockets; red fingers, black nails. Late afternoon sun, no snow today but colder, I feel it through my boots, my toes like lead but hers have got to be worse, still wearing those spike-heeled princess boots and "Cole," she says, dragging out the word, "says to wait."

A guy and girl come out of the Blue Mirror in a puff

of warm, steamy air, coffee perfume; it's Saturday, and very crowded. "He wants me to wait for him here?"

"That's what he said." Last night, with him there, I could barely see her, deep in his shadow; now I look, studying the dark mascara creases, the downward pull of her mouth, the way she shifts from foot to foot, glances from side to side, like Paz does when he's agitated. I wonder again if she's Cole's girlfriend. Skwatters tend to move less in couples than in groups, clumping and unclumping, like, what is it, atoms? or cells or microbes or something, splitting and re-forming. . . . I've never been much of a joiner. I'm more like a moon: I orbit but never touch so "I'm going inside," I say, not expecting her to follow but she does, to the only open table, a wee two-person square, too small even to open my sketchbook and I don't want to draw in front of her anyway but "You're an artist," she says, like this is an accusation, like she's caught me in some criminal act. "You go to art school or something."

"No."

She rips a napkin from the dispenser, starts to shred it, strong nervous fingers. Her nail polish is cracked and chipped. "You go to *some* kind of school."

"High school. Don't you?" though I know she doesn't, I don't know why I even said it but "No," immediately angry, she balls up the napkin shreds, flings them underhand at me. "I'm done with all that. *We're* done. We're living our own life. Cole says—" But she stops, leans back, rips out another napkin, shifts her gears. "That hat makes you look stupid. How come you don't wear makeup? You sure need it. . . . I got this eyeliner from Sapphire, you can get anything there, the clerks are so blind. Once I took this whole *display*, like, of eye shadow, I didn't even *want* it—"

"Is that where you get your lipstick?"

A hateful look, her eyes so yellow I blink, flat molten gold but "Hey," from behind me, cold hand on my shoulder and "Mags," Cole says, "you made it." Wide blue smile, a new black parka. "Let's go."

His hand a sweet weight, *go*? "Go where?" but all at once I'm buying coffees and biscotti, Jouly stuffing the cookies in her pockets, Cole with his arm through mine to lead me, us, back outside—where's Marianne? at the table still, shredding napkins, why isn't she coming?—to "The Wishing Well," Cole says. "Come on."

It's like trying to follow mercury. Skirting and sliding through the sidewalk crowds, weekend mob of shoppers and tourists and bus-stop cops, other skwatters who keep their distance, a whole waist-high flock of little kids throwing pennies into the fountain, the coins dinging dull against the ice but "Watch," Cole says, and takes from one of them a quarter, twirls it in his fingers like a TV magician, then *snap!* too fast to follow it hits the ice, splits the ice, sends up a scatter of diamonds, a spray of cold wet drops. The kids shriek and laugh, Jouly cries out "Do it again!"—

—but it's me he's looking at, gauging my smile, giving me his and "Magic," he says. "I love it. Don't you? . . . Here, give me another quarter," and he closes his hand around mine, squeezes tight and "Make a wish, Mags," he says, then with our hands still joined flings the quarter out, to spin in space, silver and cold and . . . gone.

gone

—gone where? it didn't hit the water, or the ground, I was watching, where'd it *go*? as Cole grins wide at my surprise and "It disappeared," he says. "That means we got our wish."

Our wish: but I hadn't wished for anything, or maybe my wish already came true, here by the side of the fountain, his hand still holding mine: but I don't tell him that, I don't say anything, I don't have to because now we're walking hand in hand, Jouly crunching biscotti in our wake, and he's telling me a story about last summer, sleeping out by the river, the firefly campfires, the humid scent of drugstore wine and "When the cops got there," smiling, "I was up in one of the trees, hanging up there like a, like a bird—"

"Or a bat," I say. "Bats see in the dark."

"A bat, right. . . . And I hung there and watched them kick everybody out, take them to jail, or to Sheltering Light or someplace. And they never saw me once." Leaning closer, his mouth to my ear now, his lips against my skin: a warm tickle, wonderful and sly. "Know why? Because I didn't want them to."

Stopping now right on the sidewalk, turning me to face him and "I watched you," he says, his face close to mine; his eyes are so beautiful, so incredibly deep and dark. "At the coffee place, I watched you drawing, I saw you every day. And I said, she's different. She can see."

"See what?" though I can barely hear myself, my heart is so loud and "See me," he says, and kisses me, the softest, most gentle kiss but I feel it like, like a stone dropped way down to the bottom, sending up ripples and waves, all I can do is hang on and "You're the one, Mags," he murmurs. "I knew it right away."

"How," in the wash of the waves, unbelievable, unbelievably sweet, "how do you know my name? 'Mags,' how did you—" but he's kissing me again, harder this time, tongue tip between my lips, honey-sweet—

—as "Hey!" from Jouly up ahead, "hey you guys, look at *this*!" so he, I, we join her, still hand in hand, like walking through a dream to where she stands, looking in the store window, a toy store with an elaborate display, all kinds and sizes of Raggedy Ann and Andy dolls, big as a child, small as your palm and "I used to have a Raggedy Ann," Jouly says; her eyes are so bright, for a minute I don't realize she's ready to cry. "I slept with her every night. But my dad said—"

"That one looks like Marianne," Cole says, pointing with our linked hands, a doll in the back with black hair instead of red, long scraggly corkscrews, he's laughing but "Don't cry," I say to Jouly, the dumbest thing to say to someone crying but I can't think of anything else, I can't think, period, all of me seems to be living in my hand, palm to palm, warm and cold and "You like those?" Cole says to Jouly, like he's just noticed her staring at the window. "Wait a minute."

The store's hot and overcrowded, a bunch of kids scuffling over the LEGO table, the Barbie counter swarming with little girls. At the big display—even more dolls than in the window, red banner wide above—IT'S A RAGGEDY ANN WORLD!—Cole roots through the ziggurat of dolls, plucks up one then another as I stand behind him, watching: tossing them aside, making a mess until "Excuse me," a salesperson disapproving. "Do you need some help?"

"Not from you," his smile suddenly a smirk, Jouly giggles hands to mouth and then "Come on," Cole pushing our way back to the door, the chill of the street a welcome shock, where to now? but "Here," pulling from his parka pocket a little Raggedy Ann, price tag gone from its wrist and "Thankyou thankyou thankyou!" Jouly one-armed hugging Cole, happy as a five-year-old, she looks like a five-year-old and "She wanted it," Cole says to me, shrugging.

And what can I say? *Stealing is wrong*? even though it is but the store won't miss one tiny doll, and Jouly is so happy, Cole happy to make her so, so "Yeah," I say, as he takes my hand again, "yeah she did," and we start back down the street, heading toward the Blue Mirror, the streetlights just starting to come on.

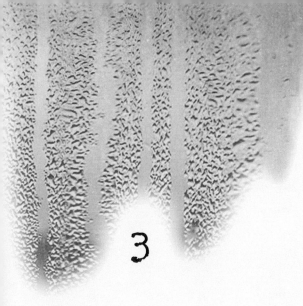

3

Way past midnight in my bedroom, Tensor light a pale lozenge on the sketchbook page, I try to get down everything that happened, hold that silver bubble in my hand. Paz sits at the window, tail whipping as he watches the street, the lurking strays, and "Paz," I say, half laughing, half pissed, "this is not *working*."

Which is totally wrong, totally backward because it should all just, just *flow*, carried on the wave of feelings, rising tide but instead it's coming out all cartoony, all pretty and arty and fake: Wishing Well splash and swoony sidewalk kisses, why can't I get him down on the page? I can see him when I close my eyes, see him in my sleep, that face. . . . At least the others are coming out OK: Jouly looks just like herself and so does Marianne, who's turned somehow into a Raggedy Ann, a Raggedy Ann with yellow cat-eyes and wild black hair, Scaryanne; wonder what she'd say if she saw it? Nothing good. *You go to art school. We're living our own life—*

—and all of a sudden my alarm's going off, six-forty, my eyes gummed shut and "Shit," I groan, Paz bright-eyed and ready for food, cold kitchen floor as I fill his bowl. Outside, it's raining or sleeting or some dismal combination, no way I'm going to school in this weather so I shuffle back to bed, Monica can just call in for me later which of course she does, she always does, squinting at me through her cigarette smoke: "Are you sick?" as I make tea for us, oolong for me, English Breakfast for her. "Are you—"

"I'm OK now," it's almost one o'clock, I got some sleep and the sleet has stopped, leaving the world glossed and sparkling. My tea steams in the travel cup; if I went downtown now, would I find him? Where does he hang out during the day? The library, the museums, the Wishing Well? or down by the river, where the homeless people go?

Sunlight now on the windowsill; Paz leaps up to its weak warmth. Monica sighs, sips her tea which she dosed with vodka, she thinks that I don't know. "You really shouldn't skip school, Maggy. You're a good student, you're smart. Don't you want to make something of yourself?"

There's no answer to that so I don't try to make one, just tuck some snacks into my bag—an apple, a granola bar—put on my boots, check my wallet, check it again: shouldn't there be more money in here? at least another five? but there isn't, just a handful of loose change in my coat pocket so "I need some cash for dinner," which starts her bitching, which makes me cranky, what right has she got to lecture me? Look how much money she wastes every week on cigarettes, not to mention alcohol. . . . I could skip all this just by going through her purse when she's asleep or passed out, but I won't do that. So we go back and forth until I'm out the door, her still yelling after—"You be back early! You hear me?"—yes, I hear you, Monica, the whole building can hear you playing mommy, which is just ridiculous. If anyone's the parent here, it's me.

A different crowd's on the afternoon bus, a different driver, a surly white guy with limp dreadlocks and a voice like a yapping dog's: "Up-front seats are seniors *only*, handicapped *only*, step to the *back*!" as I gaze out the window, wondering where to start looking, or should I just go to the Blue Mirror and wait? but the bus stop's close to the Wishing Well so I start there, the benches full, the tourists taking pictures, a couple of transit cops making their rounds.

The skwatters keep a few paces ahead of the cops, small groups melting and gelling and melting again, sharing cigarettes, eating chips, a little dirty, a little too loud. Some of them look really young, like Jouly, I wonder if they might know her, know where she, Cole, might be so "You know a girl named Jouly?" I ask one girl, too-red lipstick and chubby round cheeks, a stick-on star tattoo beneath her eye. "She's about your age, she's—"

"No," the girl says, incurious stare, turning away but "I know her," says another kid, another way-too-young one; you have to wonder about these kids' families. Doesn't anyone care that they're down here? This boy has a tattoo, too, another stick-on, BAD BOY in runny purple script. Bad boy, sure. With those big puppy eyes. "She goes around with that Cole guy. With the blue mouth. He's, like, fuckin' weird, you know?"

"What do you mean, weird?"

"*You* know. *Weird.* Like, like in a movie or something. . . . That one girl, Kyla, you know Kyla? She used to go around with Cole, she said she was his girlfriend, but then he—"

"We don't talk to nobody," says another girl, frowning, stepping between me and the boy; she's older, maybe fourteen, weary mouth and wary eyes. "We don't talk to nobody and we don't bother nobody. Come on, Jason," and she tugs him away, I watch them go but no matter who I ask about Cole, no one will really answer. They shrug, they put me off, they play dumb, but that makes sense to me since he's not just some homeless guy, some wannabe skwatter-punk; he's different. *Weird, like a movie,* well to them it probably would seem weird to see beauty in the Wishing Well ice, to take a doll to make your friend smile. All these kids care about is panhandling and getting high and acting silly; they have nothing to do with Cole.

So I head toward the river. Past the tourist part, the promenade turns from fancy brickwork to plain sidewalk, then to dead grass and mud, blown trash, the stretched and empty arms of the winter trees. Beyond that's the tent city where the homeless people live, like a grimy mushroom sprung up on the riverbank: lean-tos made of mattresses and tarps, an old swivel office chair, a bike without pedals or a seat. Two guys stoke a cut-down trash-can fire; a woman dumps empty cans into a grocery sack. It's all lonely, and kind of scary, like a refugee camp, refugees from an invisible war, why did I come here anyway? Cole's not down here, Cole wouldn't be—

—"Hey!" harsh from right beside me, comes from who knows where: Marianne, Scaryanne, still wearing Cole's green jacket, red cold sore fresh beside her blue frown. She looks tired today, her eyes slitted and dry. "What're you doing here? You don't belong here, someone'll rob your stupid ass."

I'm looking for Cole but that's none of her business, is it? though I know she knows where he is, so "Cole," I say. "Where is he?"

"How come you're not in school?"

"I didn't go today."

34   "Dumbass. You want to end up like that?" nodding backward toward the tents, someone's turned on a radio, screechy and loud: *You want it? / Go get it! / You want it? / You got it!* "Living out of a fucking garbage can? Be my guest."

Why is she always so nasty to me? I never did anything to her. "What about you?" I say, nettled. "You're not in school, you scrounge around like a—"

"We're not homeless," Marianne growls, "we're just—houseless. We have plenty of places to stay," leading me back toward the promenade, to one of the gazebos, gang signs and dog crap, graffiti faint on one side, RECKERS GO!! Inside is Jouly, curled up in a kiddy sleeping bag, pink prancing unicorns, Raggedy Ann tight in her hand and "Is this where you guys sleep?" I ask. Gritty floor, scattered candy wrappers. "Is this—"

"No, we sleep at the Plaza, in the penthouse suite. . . . You got any money?"

I think of what Monica gave me. "Not really."

"Then let's go," bending down to shake Jouly, wake her, lead us where? Back toward the Wishing Well, back to find Cole? but no, she heads straight for the shopping district, the glossy designer stores, all the competition shoppers clustered with bags—and "Wait here," Marianne says to me, depositing me in a doorway like tying a dog to a lamppost, and then scoots and shoves her way into the crowd, Jouly clumsy but determined in her wake, what are they doing? They stop short in front of people, make them stop, Jouly talks and Marianne jostles, then they dart away to do it again, do what? but then I see, know, as "Not bad," Marianne back to the doorway to flash a red leather wallet clogged with credit cards, Jouly claps her hands but "I have to go," I say. Charm bracelets and toys are one thing, but this is really stealing, you can get arrested for this. "I have to—"

Marianne smirks. "No, *you* have to go turn the wallet in. Otherwise I'll just throw it in a trash can, and somebody will find it and max out all the nice lady's credit cards. And it'll be all your fault."

"How can it be my fault? You're the one who stole it, you're—"

"Hey, we have to *live*, dumbass—"

"Hey, hey," half laughing, "girls, girls," and it's Cole, arms around me from behind; he smells sugary, like burnt cotton candy, like cookies baked just a little too long. "Mags, are you hungry? Let's go to Thai Village," down the block, using the wallet money, Cole feeding me bites of his chicken satay and telling me a long story about how they all met last fall, on the benches by the Wishing Well, in the swirl of yellow leaves: Jouly a frightened runaway, Marianne "a prisoner of war," grinning at Marianne who doesn't smile back, who looks away. "And me," who's lived, he says, all over, gypsy uptown, suburbs, even way downriver, out in the country, "which is where I learned how to sleep outside, keep warm, all that. Sometimes the country is easier. . . . But I wouldn't have met you there, would I?" and his lips brush mine, one hand on my belly, can he feel my heart? like a live thing, warm thing, hot thing leaping to get free and for the first time I really kiss him back, the wet dark sweetness of his mouth, suck at his breath like it's my own and "Mags," his murmur as I draw back, dizzy. "Oh Mags—"

Whang! Marianne flings her empty carton in the trash, bangs the lid hard and "Here," shoving the wallet across the table at me. "If you're gonna do it, *do* it," so back we go to the shoppers and the fancy stores, the one she points to even has some kind of doorman, sleek black suit and no smile at all as I approach, wallet in hand, telling myself that that kind of woman won't even miss the money, and at least she'll get her credit cards back, which is what she really cares about, right? though I know it's really bullshit, me telling me a lie but "I found this," I say to the door-man, thrusting out the wallet like it might explode; my face is so red, it might explode, too. "In the, I mean on the sidewalk."

And before he can say a word, ask a question, off I scuttle, back across the street where Jouly cheers like I just scaled a mountain, Marianne rolls her eyes, but all I'm looking at is Cole who's looking at me like no one ever has, like I'm all he wants to see, our hands locked together like one hand, one heart beating and "You're one of us now," he says. "You're mine."

His fingers are cold, I try to warm them up as we walk, aimless past the Wishing Well then down by the river as the sun sets and the stars come out, silver-white like drops of ice. Jouly yawns and shivers, Marianne mutters to Cole, who shakes his head: "No, take her somewhere. We're going back to the place."

"Take her where? I can't just—"

"Do it," head turned so I can't see his face but I see hers, a flat look, scared, scared of what? as she hooks Jouly by the arm, veers back toward the promenade as we go forward into the dark, to the graffiti'd gazebo where he opens his black parka, spreads it wide as wings and "Come here," his murmur as he draws me in, covers me like a wave, like drowning in honey, all of a sudden his mouth is everywhere, his chill and knowing hands and "Stay with me," he whispers. "Stay all night tonight, Mags."

"I can't." Night air on my breasts, is that my voice? breathless and mewing, barely there as "I *want* you," he says, nuzzling my throat. "You're mine—"

"Cole, please. Cole, *no*, OK? No," even though I want him to keep going, too, a blind soft greedy want, but I don't, I can't just—*do* this, not this way, not here in the cold and the dark so I pull back, hands shaking so I can barely button my shirt, the tiny sound of his zipper going up and "Cole," I say, but he doesn't answer. "Don't be mad, OK? I just, I—have to go." Silence; he doesn't turn. I wait in that silence, my knocking heart like a hand at the door, *Let me in, let me back in; please.* "Will you walk with me to the bus stop?"

Hands in his pockets, face a blur in the darkness like he's there and not-there, his voice as if from far away as "I can't," he says. "I have to wait for them to come back, it's not safe here. . . . Wait a minute," as I shoulder my bag, tears warm and sudden in my eyes. "I got this for you."

Something silver and slim, like a capped pen and "I'll see you tomorrow, right?" I say, voice thin as I walk backward, away from the gazebo, crunching on stones and glass but he doesn't answer and I can't stay any longer, I'll miss the last bus—which I almost do anyway, sprinting up just as the doors are scissoring shut, "Wait! *Wait!*" so they open again, grudgingly, the driver gives me a nasty look as I drop into a seat, heart thudding, hand in my pocket to pull out the silver thing Cole gave me: it's a lipstick, an Ang-Joo lipstick, expensive and creamy, called Midnight Kiss.

The window makes a kind of mirror, mirror for a ghost-face Maggy whose pale lips I line and color blue, dark blue, almost black in that aquarium light, making me into someone I've never seen before, someone straight out of "The Blue Mirror." Do I like her? this solemn, wild, dark-mouth girl? Is she me?

Midnight kiss; his coat held wide: *You're mine.* Is she? Am I?

The bus hits a bump; the mirror-girl wavers. I watch her eyes until she looks away.

4

If a stranger looked at "The Blue Mirror" now, dark skew is what she'd see, Hieronymus Bosch in a high-speed blender meets Alice-through-the-looking-glass, if Alice was sixteen and me. The designer shoppers sprint like Dr. Seuss gazelles, Scaryanne and Jouly at their heels, swift scarecrow creatures nipping and pouncing; the gazebo is battered silver, the river runs black and blue. The Wishing Well spits and spills, hearts and daggers; the sidewalks are all made of glass, or ice, too slippery to walk on but too dangerous to try to stop.

And at the center, the heart, yeah, of every page, is Cole—or where Cole would be if I could ever draw him,

my failure at which is past pissing me off, is starting to . . .
disturb me. I've spent this whole morning on just one

panel, Cole with his arms wide, dark parka spread behind
him like clouds in a sunset, I have the parka and the sunset fine but I've erased his face so many times I'm erasing
away the paper, digging a hole, why is this *happening* to
me? I've always been able to draw anything, everything:
even the time I got beat up by those kids, or the night
Monica went into the hospital, no matter what it was I
could make it real. But now—

—Paz walks across the sketchbook and sticks his butt
in my face, gazing over his shoulder with a look so incredibly feline that I have to smile, that special mix of toddler
and sphinx. "Is your bowl empty, Paz?" so I fill it with
tuna since we're out of canned food, I'll have to run to the
grocery store before I go downtown today.

As I'm scraping the can, Monica creeps in, red-eyed,
with shaking hands to fill the kettle, dose her tea and "Are
you home *again*?" all shitty and disapproving, like she's
a real mother or something. "Don't think I'm going to
keep calling in for—oh!" as I slam down the can on the
counter, Paz jumps and "I'll call for myself," I say, "and
tell them I'm you. So don't take out your hangover on me,
all right?"

She sinks into a chair, peers sideways, not quite at me.
"What's wrong with you lately?" she says in a different
voice. "I hardly ever see you, you stay out till all hours,
you're so, so—"

"So what?" but I don't wait for her answer, I don't care what she thinks, there's nothing wrong with me except I can't draw Cole—I mean I can draw someone who looks like him, the beautiful eyes and the hair, his long graceful lean, the way he tilts his head to one side. But the essential, the real *Cole* of him. . . . He wasn't mad that I couldn't stay, not really: *I just hate it when you say no to me, I can't stand to hear you say no. It's like you're keeping yourself from me.* Keep myself from him? oh never. He asks again and again to look through my sketchbook, he wants to see "The Blue Mirror," *I want to see what you've got* but how can I show him this crap? But how can I say no about this, of all things? All week I've put him off, made excuses, *later, later* but I want to show him, I want him to see everything: everything I've ever done, everything I am.

Since that first night in the gazebo—I drew some of it anyway, the stars' white tumble, the sharp, cold tears in my eyes—we've spent every single day together: sometimes with Marianne and Jouly, sometimes just Jouly, yesterday just by ourselves: first side by side at the library, on one of the straight-backed couches, me pretending to read, his sleeping head on my shoulder a precious weight, until it was time for dinner, pad thai and chicken satay, my treat. Then we panhandled by the Wishing Well, Cole made it into a game, which tourist will give us the most money? The mom-types were by far the best, folded bills and worried eyes, thinking about their own kids probably; the well-dressed younger couples were the worst of all.

Then we went down to the river, to throw stones far out where the current churns, and make dozens of wishes, the wilder the better—

I wish I had wings, huge wings like a condor. Or a pterodactyl.

I wish I could live forever.

I wish Paz could talk.

I wish you'd stay all night with me, looking not at me but into the river, the surge and crackle of the water, the pitted gray chunks of ice. I opened my mouth but before I could speak he kissed me, again and again, little hurt kisses as if he were lost, drowning, as if I were the only one who could save him. And I kissed him back, drowning myself. And I stayed.

But it wasn't how I thought it would be, I mean we didn't do what I thought we'd do: make love. Mostly we spent a long time just huddled under the sleeping bags— Jouly's ragged pink one, a new plaid polar bag—and Cole talked, long looping stories of all the places he'd been, fancy lofts and cruddy church shelters, *You can't imagine how bad they smell. Like sneakers. Dead people's sneakers.*

Why couldn't you live at home?

No answer; maybe he didn't have a home; maybe his parents were dead. Or divorced or weird or wrong somehow, I didn't press because I know how it is, I don't like to talk about Monica. And anyway he was off on something else, a litany of names, all the people he used to hang around with: Abby and Erika and Tasha, Kyla and Doucette—

Kyla?

This girl I knew, arms tightening around me; they were all girls, the people he knew, all there for a season then gone, into rehab or back home or just away, they never stayed, *they were never there when I needed them*, his hug so tight now that it hurt. *You won't leave me, will you, Mags? I need you.*

No, the word a breath, a puff of white air; squeezing the arms that squeezed me, *no never* and that was when it happened, kind of, I mean he—did things to me, with me, but not like I expected, not the way I'd hoped: touching and kissing and taking off our clothes, but it was like touching through a curtain, him on one side and me on the other, real and unreal and over so fast, all done before I'd even really started and *Next time*, blue lips yawning, *bring a condom*—and then silence, the cooling weight of his body against mine, and me wide-awake in the dark, feeling left behind somehow, and lonely, like someone stranded in an empty house.

I never slept, how could I? when it was so cold, and clammy from the river—and all the shouts and rustlings from the tent city, *it's not safe here.* . . . But when he woke up his smile was so satisfied, so sleepy-sweet, *Mags* a murmur of his lips against my heart. *You stayed.*

I'll never leave, I said.

So is it because I feel the way I do that I can't draw him? How do I feel? Am I "in love," is that what this is? the deeps and the peaks, the feeling of being chosen, like some fairy-tale girl rescued from her tower room, Prince Charming come calling at last?—but how can I figure any of it out with Monica mumbling and sniffling all over the house, she won't leave me alone so I take my tea into my room—"I have to *sleep*"—and shut the door in her face, Paz pushes it open again two minutes later but when I open my eyes again it's late afternoon and something's wrong, something's burning—

—no, something's cooking, Monica at the stove making "Spaghetti," proudly, stirring the bottled sauce. "For dinner," which actually isn't that bad, a little sticky but definitely edible but then "You're going out?" all Marmee-disappointed, one home-cooked meal heals all. "Tonight?"

"I won't be late," I say, why do I bother to lie? Maybe because she looks sad. Maybe because I feel suddenly good, bag on my shoulder, released and happy as I click the door shut, heading for the Blue Mirror to wait for Cole who's late but that's OK, OK too that I didn't get my booth because I don't need the window, do I? I'm living it now, every day with Cole is like being *in* "The Blue Mirror" and "Hey," from over my shoulder, I cover the page with my arm—a girl's wild, watchful face, the bus-window me—but it's Casey, handing me a cookie: "New vendor," he says. "Billy's Bakery, downtown. You like?"

"It's good." My lips make a blue mark on the white cookie, white-chocolate raisin. "Sweet but not too sweet."

"Just like you. . . . So where've you been, anyway?" Leaning two-handed on the table, something in his smile I can't identify. "I gotta say, I miss you, kiddo. You make this place fun."

I feel the flush, a prickly pink and "Well," I say. "I'm hanging out with Cole and those guys now, you know, and we— We spend a lot of time walking around, you know?"

"Yeah. I know. Showing you the town, huh?" as he sits down beside me, no smile at all now and "You sure about him?" quietly. "I mean, I hear stuff, Maggy. People talk."

"Talk about what? About Cole?" but he won't really say, he's vague, he's worried about me, why? but he won't tell me that, either, just "You're changing," with a dry little shrug. "You're acting different, you sure look different—" one finger to my lips, blue spot like a dot of paint left behind. Midnight Kiss; it does make me look different, kind of sallow, but cool too, I think, even though I must be putting it on wrong or something, why does mine wear off so fast and Cole's never does? even when we kiss but "I like it," I say, firmly. "I like him. And he likes me. A lot."

"Yeah, he wants you, all right. . . . Listen, Maggy, just answer me this: Who pays for stuff, when you guys go out? Who picks where you go and what you do? Huh?" I don't answer. "He's a—user, he's using you. And not just you, either."

"What's that supposed to mean?" too loud, a couple at the next table glance and grin and "He cares about me," I say, quiet but hard; *he loves me.* "He's the best friend I've ever had."

"Christ, I hope that's not true. Listen—" but "Casey, hey," from behind the counter, the manager holding out the phone so "Don't leave," Casey says to me, scooting out of the booth. "I'll be right back."

I scowl down at my sketchbook. *He's using you,* using me for what? Why is Casey saying these things? but "Maggy," Jouly's chirp, "hey Maggy," followed by Marianne in a stained jean jacket a size too small, dark marks on her cheek and chin, makeup? no they're bruises, red scrape bright beneath her eye and "Here," Marianne says, handing me Cole's old green jacket. "He'll be here in a minute, put it on."

"What happened to you? What—"

"I fell," she says; Jouly bites her fingertips, slides into the booth. "On the fucking ice, OK? On my fucking face. . . . Put it *on,*" so I do, the sleeves too long, I fold them into cuffs as here comes Cole, hands in parka pockets, he looks upset and "You," to Marianne, his voice not loud but it carries. "Come here."

"Cole," my own voice too soft, he doesn't hear, he doesn't look at me but at Marianne, who for a minute just stands there, head down, she takes a big breath then puts up her chin, crosses the café, they go outside and "Are you drawing, Maggy?" Jouly says. Nibble-nibble at her fingers. "Can I see?"

On the sidewalk across the street, I can't see Cole's face but I see Marianne's, mouth pulled low, lower, it almost looks like she might cry, Marianne crying? what is going on? and "Jouly," I say, "what's the matter? Why's Cole mad at Marianne?"

Nibble-nibble. "She got a new coat. From Rainbows."

"Rainbows?" is that a store? but then it dawns on me, "You mean Rainbows for Girls?" which is a kind of shelter, they do drug stuff there and pregnancy testing, *Get off the streets and out of the storm*, that's what the handouts say; but why would Marianne go there? "Why did she—"

"Can I draw?" reaching for my pencil, "I want to draw," but "Jouly," I say, holding the pencil away from her, like candy from a baby. "Is Cole mad because Marianne—"

"They gave us juice," she mumbles. Too many people passing by, a moving frieze between the window and the street, blocking my view. "They made Marianne pee in a cup. Like when I went to St. Ann's. They said I had a problem with boys."

"Who said? What do you—"

Nibble, giggle: "I'm a kissaholic. I like kissing boys.

But at St. Ann's they said I had a low—a low esteem. Which was how come the boys liked me!" gaily, like she'd solved a puzzle. "Cole likes me. But he doesn't kiss me anymore."

Anymore? "Jouly, what do you—" but here they come, Cole with his arm around Marianne, he's smiling but she's not, she won't look up, hands stuck in her armpits and even at the table she won't look, won't speak, only sits and shivers but "Come on," Cole says to me, as if the other two aren't even there. "I want to show you something."

Jouly scrambles out, obedient; Marianne still won't look up but "Stay here," Cole says to her, crisp, as Jouly and I rise, troop together toward the door—

—and Casey catches my eye, tries to, I see him looking but I won't look back, palm on the glass, pushing out and "Hey," Cole tenderly in my ear, "you like that jacket? It's yours now. 'Cause what's mine is yours," as the door opens and the night air hits us, lifts my hair like invisible hands, blows the trash across the sidewalk where the homeless guy lies in his plastic shroud. Through the window I see Marianne; she never looks up once.

Ice on the promenade, a gray scum underfoot, and Cole's breath a sugar cloud, free hot chocolate from the Promise House van and "As soon as I saw it," he says, "I thought of you." A painting, hung in a gallery window, lit

up and gleaming like something from church: a wild gal-
loping creature, half-woman, half-deer, smeared with red-
paint blood, and below it a little white card, *In Memory*
of Frida Kahlo, the famous Mexican artist, *like you* he'd
said as we stood there, arms around each other's waists,
links in a chain. *Like your pictures. Right?*

My pictures, I wish. This woman's force is like a can-
non, you could feel it through the glass, through the years.
I feel it again now when I close my eyes, conjure the deer-
woman's defiant face, the leap of the blood, the paint;
Cole must have felt it too. *I thought of you.*

Afterward we walked together, not talking much, slipping fluid through the sidewalk crowds: quicksilver, I'm
quicksilver too when I'm with him, faster, brighter, lighter
on my feet, even in this leaden cold that seeps through my
jacket, his jacket, our jacket. Is it being with him that does
this, or am I this way anyway and he somehow brings it
out? The magic of the prince. Fairy dust. Midnight kiss.

Now in the gazebo Jouly fools with her PROMISE
ME button, we each got one from the van: pinning it to
her coat, her hat, her Raggedy Ann, her coat again as
Marianne, reclaimed from the Blue Mirror, hunches on
the steps, hands jammed in her armpits, shivering in hard
little bursts, jerks, "You want a sleeping bag?" I ask but
she doesn't answer, she's barely said a word all night: just
trailed behind Cole and me, Cole ignoring her and Jouly
both until "Marianne," casual now, but sharp, the way

you'd call a pet you didn't love. "Go back to the van. Take Jouly."

Marianne is silent. "They won't give us any more hot chocolate," Jouly says. "Two cups apiece, that's all they ever—"

"Go on," but "It's cold," I say to Cole. "And she's not even wearing a coat, she's—"

—up on her feet now, glaring glassy-eyed at me, her bruises look almost black and "Don't," she snarls, grabbing for bewildered Jouly, stumbling away on the ice, I open my mouth to call them back but Cole's kissing me, chocolate kiss, hands in my hair and "Let her go," he murmurs. "She's fucked up anyway. Marianne's got some problems, you know?"

Tiny little kisses now, on my mouth, my eyelids, down my throat, the pleasure rising in me like mercury but "What do you mean?" I say, pulling back just a little. "What kind of problems?"

"It doesn't matter. You—"

"What kind of problems?" and he sighs, he sees I have to know so "Jealous," he says. "She's jealous of you. Because she knows I love you."

I love you, like a hot flower under my skin, I feel it blossoming all over, in my face, between my legs, he sees and says it again, "I love you," and smiles, a tilted smile, "Mags didn't you *know*?" and "No," my own voice husky, embarrassed and amazed, no one has ever, ever said that to me, I thought no one ever would—

—and he's kissing me again, hard this time, thumbs in the V of the green jacket's zipper—his jacket, mine— like peeling a piece of fruit, pulling up my sweater, hands and lips and it's so cold, hot *and* cold, *I love you* there in the gazebo, river wind and tent-city noises, someone far away yelling "OK? OK!" as the curtain between us shifts, splits, and just for a second I feel it, his hunger: enormous, resistless, *he wants you all right*, who said that? Does everyone know but me, everyone see, all I see is what I draw but here it is, right in front of me, inside me, swallowing me whole and I want to be swallowed, I want to be *consumed*, all the way down to the bones: in cold and slippery pleasure, in dark devouring heat—

—and his shuddering sigh, pressing me, pinning me back against the railing, catching his breath, my own breath cloudy white as "Mags," on another sigh, "baby, scratch my back," so I do, hands climbing beneath his coat, expecting sweat but it's cool, cool and dry and "You love me, too," he says. "Don't you," but not like a question, a lover's right, he's so beautiful here in the dark and "Yes," I whisper, a wisp of mist on the air, "of course I do," and he closes his eyes like he might start to purr, a satisfied grin like the smile on my own face, I could stand like this all night.

But at last he pulls away, pulls me down to the sleeping bag nest and "You liked that picture, huh? that painting?" he says. "I knew you would."

"It's great. *She's* great. I've read some about Frida Kahlo, and she—"

"You should do paintings. A painting of me. . . . When are you going to show me your drawings?"

The excuses rise automatic to my lips, *later, later*, but later is never unless it's now so "OK," I say, finally, and reach for my bag, drag it between us and pull out my sketchbook, my flat purse-flashlight, palm-sized light on pages of snake-necked clerks, bike messengers with wings, Scaryanne scowling at the Wishing Well as Jouly—pink chipmunk, pouty blue lips—catches diamond drops in a kid's beach bucket but "Where am I, Mags?" and so because I have to, I show him: the parka, the sunset, the tangle of his hair, I can't meet either pair of eyes, the fake empty ones I've drawn, failed to draw, or his own, how disappointed he must be—

—but "This is great," his crow, taking the flashlight from me, is he kidding? a bad joke or trying, yes, to make me feel better but we both know it sucks so "I'm sorry," I say, glancing up at last but he's not looking at me, he's staring at himself and "This is *great*," again; he means it, how can he mean it? How can he look at that, that stupid cartoon and say "It looks just like me," so "No," I say over his shoulder, the wind in my face, "no I can do better, a *lot* better. Like the way I did Marianne. Or this guy, see," a backward-walking man, belly like a pelican's beak, hat like a mushroom cap over his eyes. "I got him fine. But when I draw you—"

But Cole's not listening. "Oh, man, you have to do another one. Like this," tapping the page, "but big, right? A portrait," smiling at me but only peripherally, he won't let go of the book. "A portrait of me."

And how can I tell him, explain that I can't do a portrait of him, I can't draw him at all—but I don't have to, not yet, stuff my book back in my bag as here come Marianne and Jouly, Jouly in the lead and "Marianne is sick," she announces, eyes wide, as Cole rises, hand out, to pull me from the nest we made, from warmth into cold; bad cold. "She has to sleep someplace inside."

"Just for tonight," Marianne mumbles. She can barely talk through her chattering teeth, she shifts from foot to foot like something breaking, shuddering to a stop. "Promise House. Just for tonight," but "No," Cole says at once, "just get into the sleeping bags, you'll be fine. Jouly, you get in too, and wrap up. . . . Stupid," to Marianne, who doesn't move, "I said get in there."

"Inside. Just for—"

"What is the matter with you?" but he doesn't mean the cold, I don't know what he means but she does and so does Jouly, they're both staring at him, the flashlight wavers in my hand and "Shut that off," he says to me, not mean, not even loud but I do it immediately, we stand there breathing in the dark and "I'm walking Mags to the bus stop," Cole says. "You two stay here."

He leads me silent down the slope, the humps of dirtied snow, we don't talk until we get there and "Tomorrow," he says, "at the Blue Mirror. But not until later, like ten. I have stuff to do."

54   Pinning the PROMISE ME button on my jacket, our jacket, kissing me goodnight like it was any night, every night, I kiss him back but "Cole?" as he turns away, the bus headlights shining down the block, huge indifferent eyes. "Maybe Marianne really is sick. Maybe she needs to—"

"Oh I know what she needs," he says; I can't see his face, but I can hear his smile. "I'll see you tomorrow, Mags."

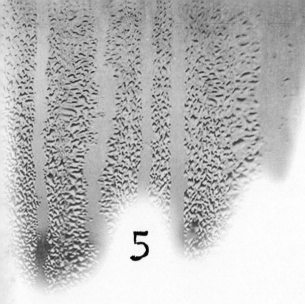

5

Morning light in my face, and still the smell, like a nasty memory, the sour odor of vodka and vomit. Last night I cleaned as best I could—I had to, exhausted or not, had to change her shirt and prop her up with pillows, make sure she wouldn't fall over and choke—but now she's done it again, big yellow splotch beside the sofa and "*Damn* it," my voice dry and furious, Paz under the kitchen table watching as I scrub my hands afterward, window wide open even though it's cold. Anything to get rid of that smell.

And now that the dirty work's done, here she comes, shuffling down the hall, holding on to the back of the chair and "Make some tea?" she croaks, blinking and squinting like some troll out of its hole. "Maggy? Tea?"

Slosh, the water, *bang* the kettle on the stove, *Just don't talk to me, Monica* but she does, of course, oh her stomach and oh her head and why did I leave her home alone when she feels so bad, don't I know she feels bad?— but I don't want to say anything, if I start I might not stop, so I just drink my tea and eat my apple, as if I'm somewhere else, back in the gazebo with Cole, why can't he see how awful those drawings are? And Marianne, he can't see her either, *she's fucked up anyway* but—

—*I love you* blooms again in me and I smile, still unbelieving, warm with a secret glow—and the sudden bright idea, maybe it's because I didn't know, before, couldn't see his love, that I couldn't draw him? But now that I do—oh I'll work all day today, I'll fix that drawing, I can't go downtown until late anyway so—

"—the window, it's freezing in here, I'm freezing!" Whacking her spoon against the table, the way a kid would, a spoiled brat demanding attention so I treat her like a brat, I snatch the spoon out of her hand and "Stop it!" right into her face, her startled eyes and gaping mouth, mouthwash odor, cigarettes. "It's open because of you, because you *smell*, you smell like *puke*, OK? So shut up!" as I fling the spoon across the room, Paz escapes in a ballet leap, Monica stares for one long second before bursting into tears, a kid's tears, noisy and gasping. Too bad. Let her cry.

I find Paz in my room, hiding under the bed, golden eyes unblinking, and coax him back out with a handful of Fishies, his favorite treat, stroke him till he jumps to settle on the bed, nesting in one of my sweatshirts. Poor Paz. I wish I could take him with me at night, I hate to leave him here with her, I hate her, blotchy face and shaking hands and "What's wrong with you?" she says, wiping her eyes with a napkin as I come back to the table, to finish the last of my tea. "You're never home anymore, you're always so—so— And school called again, they said if you don't come in and get reinstated they're going to refer us to a, a social worker, I'll have to sign papers—" Waving a new napkin, a flag of surrender, now I'm supposed to jump in and save the situation but I'm tired of being the mother so I don't say anything, just let her flounder until "Are you dropping out of school?" she says to my silence. "Is that what this is all about?"

"What do you care? Have another drink," but as soon as I say it I feel bad, I feel wrong, it's not right to throw it at her like that even if she does deserve it because she doesn't deserve it really, no one does. And she wasn't always this way, she used to be—better, a person other people looked to for help, the nursing home people, she'd come home and tell my dad about it, tired on the sofa in her uniform, but proud of herself, too: *I got Mrs. So-and-so mobile again.* What would it take to get Monica mobile again? A twelve-step program? A twenty-four-step program? My dad coming back? Who knows.

Now her gaze is on me, wet and wounded; how old she looks, old and sick and tired and "Don't worry," I say, closing the window. "I'll go talk to the counselor," Mr. Tedesco, he has a big white beard like Santa Claus. "I'll straighten it out."

"Today?" hopefully. "Will you go today?"

Today I'm going to draw, for Cole tonight, so "Tomorrow," I say, taking my mug to the sink, ignoring the sky-high pile of dishes. "I'll go tomorrow."

"OK," hope melting into gratitude, a smile of pure relief, "OK, baby, that's fine." Cigarette automatic to her mouth but with a guilty glance at me she puts it down unlit, empty hands wandering up to her hair and "I'm going to take a shower," she says, like someone else might say *I'm going to climb Mount Everest*. "Can I use some of your shampoo?"

"Go ahead."

She wanders into the bathroom, I head back to my room, to a clean sketchbook page, starting with those amazing words, *I love you*, up above like skywriting, soft white tendrils of cloud. Beneath is the Promise House van, PROMISE ME on my jacket as green as spring grass, new growth that as I draw grows wild, turns dark, dark green vines reaching for the sky, the words in the sky—

—as below on the street Jouly crouches like Paz when he's scared, and Scaryanne is a snowman, snowgirl, crooked black hat and mirrors for eyes, mirrors reflecting Cole's gaze, dark and true, *I love you*—

—but as beautiful as he is, and he is, still he's grinning, not smiling, long teeth as white as the clouds, not quicksilver but steel and worse than a cartoon, much worse, oh not my Cole at all—

—so I slam the book shut and shove myself under the blankets, love is making me stupid or blind or something, or maybe I just need to sleep, sleep like deep water to carry me down. Once or twice I wake, to TV sounds, Monica's chuckle, footsteps down the hall; does the door open and close? Maybe. Paz comes and goes, curling on my legs, paw-patting my face, scampering through the dreams I have and don't, and when I wake again there are shadows on the wall, late afternoon, and Paz is digging a hole in the bed, demanding to be fed. And Monica's gone.

It's not time for a doctor's appointment, did she go to the liquor store? She's tidied up the living room, newspapers in a little pile, ashtrays wiped clean, some kind of air freshener sprayed around or maybe it's perfume, too sweet, like a ten-foot plastic flower but at least it's better than the vomit smell. I feed Paz, but there's not much to fix for my dinner, some macaroni, that salty canned ham I hate, so I just make more tea and sit at the table, thinking about Cole, about seeing him tonight, late, *I have stuff to do*, what stuff? He didn't tell me. Is it something to do with Marianne? What's wrong with Marianne? *Jealous. Because she knows I love you. I love you. You love me, too.* Yes. I do.

When I climb out of the shower, it's after seven, dark,

and Monica's home with dinner: take-out Chinese, a dozen little cartons, lo mein noodles, egg rolls, a feast, even Paz eats some when I scrape off the sweet-and-sour sauce. She's turned off the TV in favor of the radio, some funky Tex-Mex tunes; the kitchen light is bright, the room glows.

"What's your fortune?" Monica asks, cracking her cookie. "Mine says 'Your lucky day is Monday and the number seventeen.' "

"Mine says 'Stay out of the rain. Your lucky number is five.' "

Monica squints at the window. "It's raining right now. That means you should stay home," but of course I have to go, down to the Blue Mirror and "I might be late tonight," I say, plate to the sink, topping off Paz's water bowl; she did the dishes, too. "Don't worry."

"Where are you going?"

"Downtown. Don't worry," but "I do worry," she says, softly, not looking at me, twisting her paper fortune. "I don't know where you go at night, or what you do. . . . That green jacket, it's not yours, is it?"

"It is now."

"I know you didn't buy it."

You don't know anything but I don't say that, I don't answer, just get ready to go and "I'm afraid for you," Monica says. In the overhead kitchen light she looks not old but young, weirdly young, like a child without a mother. "You're changing, and I'm afraid."

"Don't be."

"Are you—is it a boy?" but "Don't worry," I say again, more kindly this time, and then I'm gone, over and out, crooked lines of rain on the smeary bus windows, my hands in my pockets, stiff with cold—but my Blue Mirror booth is open, grande cappuccino and my sketchbook, watching the street like old times.

But it's not like old times, something's different, better than before, better than ever: like X-ray, Z-ray vision, the shadows are alive to me now, shadow within shadow, showing me what was always there but I never saw so clearly before: the raptor's shrug one gang guy gives another, waiting there at the curb; the wash and eddy of rain in the gutter, the floating boats of trash and crap; that couple walking past, teddy bear and grizzly, she's planning on eating him alive later, nothing left over but the bones.

And while I'm sitting here watching all this, entranced, like it's a show put on just for me "Hey," in my ear, Casey sliding into the booth and "Hey," again, like I might not have heard him. "Maggy. How's it going?"

"Good," at once and too fast, a self-conscious, half-assed little smile, "it's good." I make the smile bigger, but it feels funny, I feel funny, artificial somehow, like what I can say and what I will say are two different things—but how can I feel this way about Casey? who just sits there looking at me, no smile, new black golf shirt and "You got your hair cut," I say, to say something: almost a buzz cut, all the spikes and tendrils gone, he runs a hand across

it and "Yeah," with a shrug. "Makes me look more man-
agerial, don't you think?"

"You're—you mean you got promoted?"

"Mm-hmm. Starting next week. It's just temporary,
Jake's helping open a new store. But if I do a good job,
they might give me this place." He runs his hand across
his hair again. "Or maybe the one up in Northwood, I
don't know."

I sit up straighter; my voice is suddenly too loud. "You
mean you wouldn't be here? You'd *leave*?"

"Things change." That soft gray gaze, half chal-
lenging, half sad. Hand through his hair again, a nervous
gesture. "Like you did, right? New lipstick, new friends.
. . . The other one was in here earlier, I think she was
looking for you. The beat-up-looking one."

"You mean Marianne? She's not beat-up, she fell." *On
my fucking face*, black and red. "On the ice."

"Yeah?" I can see he doesn't believe me. "She looks
pretty sick, too. Maybe her boyfriend doesn't take very
good care of her. Maybe he—"

"He's not her boyfriend, he's—"

"Your boyfriend, yeah, I know. . . . How's the art
coming?" tapping my sketchbook cover, like he's changing
the subject but I know he's not, he's about to say something awful, something I don't want to hear so "Casey," I
say, urgent, "you don't understand about Cole. He's not
what you think, he really cares about me, he—"

But he's got his hand up, *stop* like a traffic cop, he's

sliding out of the booth and "You've made up your mind," he says, gazing down at me with a look I can't decipher, for a split second I think of Monica, why? "I'm not going to argue with you, Maggy. Just remember I'm your friend, OK? Always your friend." He taps the sketchbook again. "And keep on drawing. No matter what else you do, keep drawing."

And that's that, he walks away before I can stop him, before I can say *Cole loves me, you don't understand* but nothing I say will make him understand, will it? He's made up his mind, too, so what can I do except slap open my sketchbook, pencil to paper, *keep drawing*, well I will: I'll draw the new unimproved going-away Casey, with his boot-camp haircut and closed-down mind, he thinks Cole, what? beat Marianne up? That's ridiculous, worse than ridiculous, she just *fell*, she said she fell—

—on the ice, in the cold, shivering, where did she end up sleeping last night? and was Jouly with her when she came in here, looking for me, *his old girlfriend, Cole doesn't kiss me anymore*, so that means Jouly, too? . . . Oh this is all *stupid*, I'll just ask Cole and he'll tell me, he'll explain as soon as he gets here, *later, like ten. I have stuff to do.* What stuff?

I know what she needs.

My drawing hand stops moving: underneath is a hard black snarl.

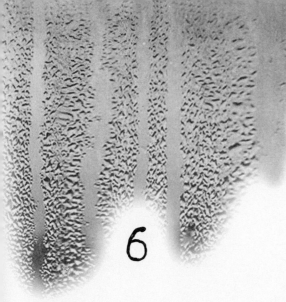

6

Now I ghost my way down the hall, school hall, it seems like a million years since I've been here: everyone's a stranger, I keep losing my way, I can't even remember half the rooms. Like I'm a refugee from "The Blue Mirror," picture-girl lost and wandering in Reality, where everything is so totally unreal.

And I'm so *tired*. Last night I never slept at all, wondering what happened to Cole, why he never came to meet me. Hunched at the table with the dregs of my cappuccino, ten o'clock, past ten, the Blue Mirror closes at eleven but Casey let me stay until he finished, midnight and locking up, slipping on his coat, did I want a ride home? but *No*, I said, furious, ashamed, *no, I'll get the bus* but *You missed your bus* so I climbed into his car, a neat rusted-out Toyota, silent all the way except for directions; I thought he would say something, rub it in but he didn't which was almost worse, like we both knew what the deal was so no one had to say a word.

But where *was* Cole? Had he just—forgotten me, blown me off? No, I can't believe that. So what happened, then? Was Marianne really sick? Did he have to take her to a shelter, or the emergency room, or something? Or was it something even worse, oh God, don't let anything happen to Cole. Please God, oh please don't let it be Cole—

—as the tone goes, the halls empty out, I don't even remember why I'm here but as some jock in a letter jacket jostles past me—"Hey look *out*"—I see behind him STUDENT CENTER, counselors this way, sign-in sheet so I sign in and sit, the PROMISE ME button in my hands, turning it over and over, thinking of Cole with a longing like physical pain: promise me, *I love you*, promise me, Cole, where were you, where are you—

"—gret? Margaret Klass?" Looking down at the card, up at me, Santa Claus in a baggy dark-brown suit, marching penguins on his tie and "How're you doing, Margaret?" as he leads me down the little hall; matte gray carpet, pale green walls. Soothing colors for overwrought teens.

"It's Maggy," I say. "I'm fine."

"Maggy, sorry," as we turn into his office, big desk, dusty silk plant in the corner; my chair squeaks, his doesn't. "I called Mom again this morning, Maggy."

Whose? yours or mine? but there's no point in getting snippy so "That's why I'm here," I say, shifting in the chair; *squeak, squeak*, like some trapped metal beast. My eyes are so tired, they ache, a gritty ache, like someone filled my sockets with sand. "I need to get, what's it called? Reinstated?"

"Ideally Mom should be here, too." Pulling up my file, swiveling the monitor so I can see it, full disclosure: UN-EXCUSED, UNEXCUSED, UNEXCUSED, bright green all the way down the screen and "There are various ways we can go here," says Mr. Tedesco, turning the monitor back. "We can talk with Alternative Education, or the PsychServ worker—"

"I'm not crazy."

"No one says you are." If this were "The Blue Mirror" he'd be a penguin, dark suit and white beard, little flipper hands crossed across his sloping belly. "But you're not coming to school, Mar—Maggy, and we need to address that. Are you having problems here? Harassment, bullying, things like that? Or is the problem at home?"

Which way would work better, get me out of here faster? But I'm so tired and it's so hard to think, I keep fingering the PROMISE ME button as he keeps talking, *social worker, suspension, get Mom in for a conference* and "My mother," I say, "is kind of—sick. Sometimes I have to stay home to take care of her. . . . Can't I just make up the work I'm missing, and, and go back to class?"

Mr. Tedesco makes a note. "I'm sorry to hear about your mother. Your father is—?"

"He lives in Iowa. Or Idaho. I don't know," and just like that I'm crying, I don't mean to but it all hits at once, Cole and the long night's worry, is he hurt? sick? mad at me for something, what did I *do*? as Mr. Tedesco hands me tissues, would I like a glass of water? but "Can't I just go back to class?" Wiping at my eyes. "Can't I—"

"Just a minute," with a professional smile, a few more notes, taking a form from a pile on his desk and then "Go on to your next hour," he says, handing me the form: *Susan Galliano, Student Outreach*. "And go see Ms. Galliano at the end of the day. Do you know where her office is?"

I don't, but I nod, nod like a magic password to get me out of there, back into the hall that smells like paper, dust, and feet, left and right and right again until I find a girls' bathroom, sit in a stall with my head in my hands, lipstick smears and graffiti, TULEY IS A HORE, what am I doing here anyway? I don't belong here, I belong downtown, looking for Cole.

By the time the tone goes off again, I'm out of the stall, eyes red but face washed, hair brushed, bag on my shoulder to walk into my next hour which is just around the corner, language arts: and see a sub, thank God, some skinny guy with red hair and a Superman tie, what is it with teachers and ties? A few kids stare as I take a seat but no one really cares enough to make a comment, Maggy the Invisible; the important thing is that I'm marked "present," and the hour passes OK.

Next hour is pre-calc so of course I'm totally lost, just sit there frowning at my book, which might as well be written in Urdu for all the good it does me. When the tone goes off, the math teacher—Mr. Knox, gold glasses and ear hair—motions me to stay, there's a ton of makeup work, *Stop by after school for tutoring, we'll get you right back up to speed* and I nod, nod, nod, lunchtime now and I'm starving, I haven't eaten since, when? that Chinese food last night? A million years ago, a million more until tonight, why does school have to take so *long*? More classes after lunch, *and* math tutoring, *and* Susan Galliano, whoever she is so "Forget it," I say out loud, and take my lunch—Hershey's bar and herbal tea, Desert Lime, astringent and sweet—down the stairs and past the parking lot where people smoke and chatter, jockettes and leather punks and skwatter-wannabes, all of them so foreign to me, all of them so . . . flat, so much less real than the people I draw, "Blue Mirror" people alive and living on the page.

So I walk and keep walking, out of the unreal and back into the world, my world, my street where with my tired eyes, my X-ray, Z-ray vision, I see everything in hyper-clarity: the blue-white sky like paper fresh for drawing; the sparrows' surge and settle, like particles, like thoughts; a grinning genie on the side of a delivery truck, WE APPEAR LIKE MAGIC!—

—and Cole

—*Cole? Yes*, waiting out in front of my building, appearing like magic, like a genie, a wish come true—

—and I don't even know I'm running till I stop, rush into his arms like two magnets clicking, sticking, he hugs me till I can't breathe and "Mags!" kissing me, hard sharp nippy little kisses. "Where were you?"

Where was I? but I can't say it, I can't say anything, I'm too relieved, too happy just to see him, see that we're OK, he's OK—but tired, he looks terribly tired, worse even than me and "It's cold out here," he says. "Aren't you going to invite me in?"

In? to my *house*? but he's waiting, head to one side, hand on the door, so in we go, climbing the stairs, his arm around my shoulder, leading me like he already knows the way and "How did you know," I say, "my address, how did—" but now we're on my floor, at my door, obnoxious TV bleat and "My mother," I start, and stop, how to explain Monica? so I don't even try, just "My mother's home," I say, and turn the key.

Cigarette smoke and a startled smile, she's woozy but not technically drunk: shifting on the sofa, turning the TV down, "Well hello," and staring at Cole, so beautiful and ragged in his lipstick and parka, so—strange, here, fierce exotic beast like a lion in the living room, quicksilver slippery in an old tin can: "This is Cole," I say, and he takes it from there, sitting right next to Monica and talking like he's known her forever, it's so nice to finally meet her, I've told him lots about her—which isn't true but she doesn't know that, she's smiling, she's hanging on every word.

So I head into the kitchen, because I don't know what else to do: be a hostess, go get drinks. A Coke for him, a Coke for me, down the hall again like walking in a fun house, where all the walls are tilted and the windows are two-way, how weird that he should be here, both halves of my life come together in one place—

—and "—sisters," he's saying as I step into the room, "you two look so much alike. I mean, you seem so young," and Monica laughs this breathless little-girl laugh, a giggle really, he's really laying it on thick but it's just what she wants to hear, apparently, she's practically purring, like Paz, where is Paz? and "Maggy wants to show me her drawings," Cole says, graceful off the sofa; I hand him his Coke, he sets it aside. "I bet you're really proud of her, being an artist and everything. Does it run in the family?"

"I suppose it does," says Monica. "I used to draw." *Monica? Draw?* When was this? "Not—nothing like Maggy does. Just little pictures of—nature, you know, trees and birds and—"

"I knew it," Cole says, and takes me by the hand, leads me down the hall to my room where the instant the door shuts he's kissing me, hard kisses, hands running up my shirt but "Not here," my murmur, "Cole no, not here—" but "She's not listening," he says, white teeth, that perfect lipstick grin. . . . and my own mouth colorless, wordless, how can I say no when I missed him so, when he wants me so much?

But in here it feels—wrong, somehow, dirty and hurried and forced, alert for any noise from the living room, back tense against the door as I wait, eyes closed, for him to be done, to zip up, to plop down on my bed in the midst of the mess and "It's nice here," he says, smiling up at me. "I think I'll move in."

Climbing next to him, shucking my shoes and "Where were you last night?" I say. "I waited and waited, I was at the Blue Mirror till midnight—"

"Well I," and he yawns, a huge pink yawn, "was walking around going crazy." Pulling me close to snuggle with him, his arm's on my hair so I try to tug it free but "Lie *still*," he says, and holds me tight, so I can't move. "I'm trying to tell you something."

"My hair's caught—"

"All *right*. Jesus. Will you be quiet now and listen?" to his story about last night, his long cold walk from the river uptown, then to the Wishing Well, then back to the river "looking," with another yawn, "for Jouly," who'd been spirited off by Marianne on some misguided rampage, missing now—

"Missing? What do you mean?"

"I mean I can't *find* her, Mags. 'Cause she's *missing*,

get it? . . . It's always like this," on a sigh. "I keep telling
them and telling them, those shelters are dangerous, you
can get raped there. Kyla was raped," solemn, his gaze
holding mine like a warm hand, caressing, enclosing. "By
this older guy. . . . He really hurt her, they had to send her
to a hospital upstate."

*Kyla, she used to go around with Cole, she said she
was his girlfriend.* "Was Kyla your girlfriend then? Was
she—"

"No, I just, I used to look out for her, you know? try
to show her things, where to sleep, how to hustle the
tourists. But she didn't listen. And now Marianne's doing
the same stupid shit. Getting Jouly all wound up, all
scared and everything. . . . I just want us to keep together,
you know?" Together in the gazebo, Jouly and her Raggedy Ann, *kissaholic, a low esteem* and suddenly my eyes
fill with tears, poor Jouly, as he shakes his head: "They're
all like that, street girls, skwatters—they're dumb, right? I
try to help them, watch out for them. But they don't listen. . . . You're not like that, are you, Mags?" leaning over
me, a closed-mouth kiss, so hard I feel his teeth behind his
lips. "You won't do that shit, you love me."

The TV turns quiet, then loud again; I think of Monica out there, listening? trying not to listen? so "Let's go,"
I say. "Let's go look for her right now."

"But it's warm here," with a smile, another pink
yawn: and it *is* warm, enveloping warmth like a cocoon,

chrysalis of blankets and coats, the fake fur of his parka's hood is soft against my cheek. "And I didn't sleep all night," me neither, so when he closes his eyes I close mine, just for a minute, just feeling him close, the empty ache I carried all day gone as if it had never been, smothered in his nearness, his closeness smoothing out all thoughts and worries, transfusion of purest warmth—

—and when I wake up it's to his gaze, those eyes I loved before I even knew him, his faintest, sweetest smile and "It's so nice to sleep inside," he says, as I blink, sunset shadows fading from the wall, we must have slept for hours. "But now it's time to go."

Kitchen sounds, is Monica making dinner? oh I hope not—but no, just the kettle, she's smiling her Marmee-smile: "Does anyone want some tea?" as Cole turns for the bathroom like he knows exactly where it is, running water and "He's darling," Monica murmurs. "Does he go to your school?"

I shake my head; the idea of Cole at school, any school, is too strange to contemplate, it's strange enough that he's here—but school, oh ugh, Susan Galliano, *get Mom in for a conference*, do I tell Monica about all that or just wait for them to call? Oh why bring it up now, when she's happy and so am I, tomorrow is plenty of time—

—and I feel something against my leg, tentative and warm, "Paz?" emerging from under the table, has he been there all this time? Ears back and peeking, nervous with a stranger in the house—but Cole's not a stranger, or anyway he won't be for long, his steps approaching as "Come here, Paz," my croon. "Come here, baby, come on—"

"Spaz?" Cole laughs, leaning in the kitchen doorway. "You call it Spaz?"

—as Paz takes one look at him and just, just *implodes*, frantic scramble back under the table, a miserable howling growl and "Paz!" me on my knees, reaching, "Paz what's the—*ow!*" Jerking back as he lashes out, long gouge across the meat of my thumb, deep enough to bleed, he's never scratched me, ever—

—and Cole takes one step, two, very fast, foot out and "Don't!" I cry, was he going to *kick* him? Kick *Paz*? "Don't, he's just scared, he's never seen you before—"

And now Monica's dithering around, paper towel for the blood, *oh dear oh the cat* and "I'm fine," I say, furious. "Let's just go."

Silent down the stairs, down to the bus stop, I forgot my gloves but I'm not going back to get them. On the bus I hunch by the window, shoulder to the glass, gaze down but "Let me see," Cole says, and unwraps my hand, sticky paper towel, still bleeding a little but he brings it to his lips, his mouth to the cut, a feeling like pressure and "There," he says. "All better."

I stare at my hand, at the cut just a pink line now, all the blood gone: it looks like it's healed, it feels like it's dead, a numb warmth, and "What did you do?" I say, wiggling my fingers. "You squeezed it, you— What did you *do*?"

Streetlights striping his face, dark and white and dark again, he smiles but doesn't answer, doesn't say anything until we get off the bus and "We should go to the Wishing Well first," I say, "or maybe the gazebo, see if they're there," but "I'm hungry," he says, and heads straight for the Blue Mirror, which is crowded but not crowded enough to keep Casey from seeing us right away, he turns his back but not before I catch his eye: sad and remote, like I'm someone he once knew, someone who left a long time ago—

—and all at once I can't stand it, I don't want to feel this way, I have to say something so I turn for the counter, Cole right behind me, to wedge through the busyness and lean over, across the cornucopia spread—all kinds of cookies in paper sleeves, a dozen wrapped sandwiches— and "Casey," I call, urgent. "*Casey*, hey—"

—as Cole presses behind me, against me, hands in my pockets, why? as Casey turns, his gaze first for me but then for Cole, his eyes icing over, like the frozen gray water in the Wishing Well and "You better go," he says, to me? No, to Cole. "Just get out of here, all right?"

Cole doesn't answer, only waits, one hand on my shoulder now, his beautiful mouth a smirk and "Stop it," I say to them both. "Don't do this—" stretching, reaching forward, reaching out for Casey—

—and as I do, out of my pocket, my left pocket, falls one of the wrapped sandwiches, *plop* on the counter, I stare at it, I don't understand until "Out," Casey says, hard, stepping around the counter as the people in line stop and stare, "both of you," out to the sidewalk where he reaches roughly into my pockets, both pockets, frisking me as more customers watch through the window, through the Blue Mirror, like it's a picture, a show: fishing out another sandwich, a cookie, a wad of paper napkins and "Don't come back," he says, as if I'm just some shoplifter, as if he doesn't know me at all. "If I see you again, I'm calling security."

"Casey—Casey I didn't *do* this, you know I didn't, I didn't even *know*—"

—but he's already gone, back inside where people sit staring at me, at Cole who stands there unconcerned, gazing at traffic as if nothing's happened or if it did, it didn't happen to him, as if nothing can touch him and "Come on," he says in his normal voice, stepping graceful off the curb. "Let's try that Coney Island on Montcalm, they're so stupid they don't even— What? What's wrong?"

"What's *wrong*?" as passersby swerve around us; my voice is high and loud, like something stretched too far. "Cole, Casey thinks I stole that food! He thinks—"

"Who cares what he thinks? Besides," grinning like it's all a big joke, "it's your own fault, Mags. If you hadn't been bending over that way—"

"My fault! You're the one who put it in my pocket—"

"I was hungry," annoyed, as if that should be obvious. "Anyway it's just a couple of sandwiches, what's the big deal?"

How can he not know this? not *see*? "The big *deal* is I can never go back in there," the Blue Mirror ten steps away but it might as well be ten miles, a million: never see Casey or explain to him, never sit in my booth again, the Maggy Klass Memorial Booth, the window my mirror to show me, what? that Casey thinks I'm a thief now? that Cole—"The big *deal* is you made me steal from my friend!"

"Friend?" Eyebrows up, a mocking half-smile. "He said he was going to call security on us, what kind of a friend is that?"

"What kind of friend makes you steal?" I can hear the tears in my voice, feel them hot in my eyes; my voice is getting louder. I remember the toy store, Jouly and the Raggedy Ann; the red leather wallet, *you're one of us now, you're mine*. "And you were going to hurt my cat, too, you were going to—"

"Screw your cat. I fixed your hand, didn't I?" Arms crossed, he seems taller somehow, glowering at me as if from up above, way up where no one can go, no one but him and "I do a lot for you, Mags," he says. "I found you, I helped you—"

"My hand is—"

"—I love you," as if I hadn't spoken, as if he couldn't hear: one finger pointing, tapping the PROMISE ME button pinned to my jacket, his jacket, *what's yours is mine* and "I thought you were different," he says, "you're an artist, you're going to do my portrait. But if you think—"

"Look!" behind him, a blur halfway down the block but I know right away that it's her, jean jacket and snarly hair—and I wave, wild semaphore, "Cole, there's Marianne—Marianne, hey!" but she sees us, pivots, sprints, I start to rush after her but "Wait a minute," Cole hauling me to a stop, "don't chase her. *Don't*," as I struggle, oh she's getting away, jean-jacket speck blending in with the crowd, confetti blown away on the wind but "You'll never catch her that way," he says, "she runs like a fucking deer. . . . Now that I know she's still here, I'll go after her myself. But not with you," firmly. "You're going home."

"Home? I'm not going home, I'm—"

"How many times do I have to tell you? She hates you, she won't come to me if you're around. But if I'm alone—" His gaze goes past me, hunting its way through the crowd; his hands squeeze my shoulders, release to squeeze again. "Don't worry, Mags. I told you, I'll take care of Marianne."

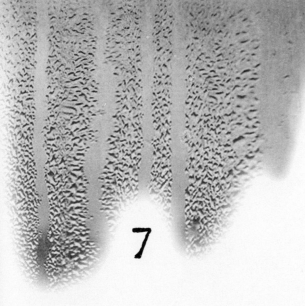

7

But I did worry. And I didn't go home, I'm not home now, I'm here: by the Wishing Well in the warm sunshine, really warm, as if overnight someone threw the winter's-over switch. The fountain is more water than ice today, the pigeons settle and wheel, the skwatters take off their coats and turn their faces to the light. And I sit here on the bench and draw it all. Just like old times.

Except it's not like old times, it's like no-times, like everything's turning even more unreal: me, the Wishing Well crowd, "The Blue Mirror," Cole. . . . The cold is still a part of me, last night's cold like lead spread under my skin, yet my feet burn from walking: shelter to shelter, all the ones I know of or can find, Good Shepherd to Sheltering Light to Promise House to Rainbows for Girls, asking *Have you seen them?* Snarly hair and Raggedy Ann, Marianne and Jouly disappeared like the snow on the ground, just melted away, but how can that be? I mean, I know skwatters come and go, you'll see a face for weeks and then never again, but I just saw Marianne last night, *she runs like a fucking deer* but where? *The other one was in here earlier, I think she was looking for you. . . . all wound up, all scared and everything.* Scared of what? Where are you, Marianne? besides the pages of my sketchbook, Scaryanne with deer's antlers, wild cat's eyes gleaming in the dark as she runs, runs, Jouly a little pink ghost on her back, running away, from what? And why do I care?

I didn't think of that last night. All I thought, as I checked out the shelters—the people in line or bedding down, skwatter-girls Marianne's age, my age, is she my age? The street makes you seem older, look older, like the girls in line, chipped nails and bulging purses, wary and weary and sly; and the younger ones, some with a parent, a mom, but most without, cigarettes and lipstick but still young and scared, in the line for the bathroom, in the smell of sweat and grimy clothes, gazing at me with round, exhausted eyes as *I'm looking for my friends*, I said, kept saying—because that was what I was thinking, even though Marianne isn't my friend, doesn't want to be, *she hates you* but I wanted to find her; I still do. Find her and—

—then what? I *had* thought of that, there in the odors and the warmth, the dead-bolt doors with their fortress feeling, sometimes you need a fortress. . . . But what would I do when I found them? or they found me? Or Cole found all of us? I didn't know. I just wanted to find them, to ask, are you OK? Just to—see.

After the shelters, the head shakes and the shrugs—*no, haven't seen them sorry no*—I just kept walking, aimless, not wanting to give up but not knowing what else to do or where to go. I ended up back at the Blue Mirror, its doors closed, shut tight for the night; drawing it now I'm just a shadow on the page, an outline looking in, hands pressed dark to the glass, face a smear, the way you see through tears. Inside are stacks of sketchbooks, and lounging, dancing creatures, and floating wisps of fragrant steam; and sandwiches, a pile of them, all made of skulls and crossbones: *Poison; keep away.* Too late—

—much too late, then, to keep on walking, too deserted on the mausoleum streets so I trudged back to one of the shelters, Good Shepherd which was closest, waited forever to use the pay phone to call Monica: four rings, five, seven, was she pissed off? or passed out smoking on the sofa, smoldering ash and Paz trapped, *Monica come ON* until finally *Maggy?* drunk but wide awake, why? and she's got a million questions, where in the world am I

and am I with my boyfriend and do I know my cat is going crazy—

What do you mean, going crazy?

*He's crying at the door, scratching and scratching,
should I let him out or—*

NO, don't let him out, I'll—what? but I couldn't tell
her, I couldn't think, tired and rushed from the line behind
me, the woman right behind me, alcohol breath and mut-
tering *Hurry up hurry up!* so *I can't talk now, I have to
go—*

*Go where? Aren't you coming home at all, don't you
live here anymore? And what about school*— as I hung
up, click and gone and back to the "lobby" (two stained
plastic lawn chairs, a poster of Jesus with a sheep) where I
hunched sideways and dozing to wait out the last of the
dark, even though all the beds were full they wouldn't
kick me out, at least not until seven a.m., rise and shine
for coffee and a bagel, another long shuffling line, girls
and women scratching themselves and yawning and
hauling their kids by the hand, the women the girls on
fast-forward, *this is what happens when you never go
home*—but at least it was better than walking the streets
all night, freezing; hiding; from what?

The wind from the river; I didn't go down there, to the
gazebo, I didn't look. *It's not safe here*, in the shadow of
the tent city, wandering, wondering if I'd see Cole, cross
his path while he searched for Marianne; I hoped I would,
I hoped I wouldn't, I wanted to climb into his arms, I

wanted to shake him and make him explain, explain, explain what went wrong, what's happening between us. . . .
How can he be one thing and then something else? How
can he be so beautiful, so everything I want, my dark
Prince Charming, *make a wish, Mags*—and then turn
into, what? What are you really, Cole?

There's a kind of answer growing on the page, under
my hand: the one Paz scratched, the one Cole "fixed,"
what exactly did he do to it? Numb, not cold but like
novocaine, clumsy like a mannequin hand—but I can still
draw, drawing him now, hair face eyes, it's starting to
come to me, *through a glass darkly*, who said that?
Through "The Blue Mirror," the mirrors of his eyes—

—"Hey," hoarse behind me, the pencil jumps, little
graphite scar and "Where's Cole?" a hiss in my ear: Marianne. "Where is he? Is he here?"

"No," half turning, "I don't know, I—*oh*," as I get a
good look at her, a bad look, what the hell *happened*?
Bruises fading now to shadows, hair snarled stiff like
meringue, ratty cardigan over the jean jacket smeared and
spotted with some kind of paint, brown paint—but it's her
eyes that scare me, wild cat with its back to the wall, kill
or die, like Paz last night as "Where is he?" gripping my
wrist, her fingers locking like a handcuff. "Where—"

"I don't know—stop it, you're hurting me! Marianne,
what hap—"

"You fucking liar," squeezing tighter, nails sharp
against my skin. "I know you know, you better tell me—"

"I don't know! I haven't even seen him since last night," and I tell her in a few words what happened, how I, we, glimpsed her on the street, what Cole had said and "That's the last I saw him," I say. "He said he was going to look for you."

She lets me go, sticks her hands into her pockets; the cardigan smells, a smell I can't identify, like old food, spoiled meat. "So what'd you do then? Run back home to mommy?"

"I went around the shelters."

Narrowed eyes, not trapped-cat but pure suspicion. "What for?"

"To look for you. And Jouly. Where is Jouly?" but she shakes her head and looks away, at the skwatters clustered at the edge of the plaza, maybe a dozen, smoking and laughing and shoving each other and "What happened?" I say, making room on the bench. "Did Cole—do something to her? Did he—"

"You got any money?"

"Marianne, you have to tell me—"

"I don't have to tell you anything! I don't have to do anything but get the fuck out of here, that's all I have to do!" and all of a sudden she's crying, weird dry coughing sobs, blue mouth stretched to an aching O and I don't even think, I just put my arms around her: it's like holding a board, tight and stiff, the bad smell from the sweater but then she just—collapses, folds in on herself, hunched against me like a little girl and "Marianne," I say into her ear; I have tears in my eyes. "How did you get hurt? Did Cole do that?"

"No. No! I told you, I fell on the ice." Pulling away from me, wiping her face with her sleeve—and all of a sudden she's off the bench, on her feet again and ready to run but I hook her arm and slew her back down, she's strong but I'm stronger, I won't let her go, I have to know so "Sit down," I say, my face an inch from hers. "And tell me."

She sits, she wipes her face again, she stares at her hands, filthy hands and "Tell you what? I fell on the ice, by the gazebo, I was trying to get away. I've been trying for a long time."

"Get away from what?" but somewhere in me, like a drawing I can't see, I already know, I know that I know even though I don't want to, don't want to hear what she's saying but it's too late, now that she's started she won't stop: "I was hanging around in that café, you know? selling shit to those rich girls? And I saw you there, drawing, and when you went to the bathroom I took a look," nodding to my sketchbook, still lying open on the bench. "I saw your drawings, and the name, *mags*, you know? And I thought it was cool, so I told him. . . . I didn't mean anything, I swear to God. I never thought he'd go after you."

The sun in my eyes, burning; I squint, squint her into a scarecrow, a witch, wicked and jealous and "Lying," my own abrading whisper, like sandpaper, like rust. "You're jealous, you— *He* saw me first. He *wants* me—"

"I know. He wants me, too. He wants all of us. I just didn't think you were the type to—"

"What type? What are you talking about?"

She's holding my hands now, as hard as I'm holding hers, I feel it from far away and "The loser type," she says, bitterly. "That's what he always goes for, right? The losers, the lonely ones away from the herd. Like me. And Jouly. . . . At first it's great, he's all over you, he loves you, he tells you what to do, right? But then he gets—inside of you somehow, he— Like those nature shows, you know? how they gut a polar bear or something when they need to hide from the cold? That's how he is. That's Cole."

Silence, between us. The sound of the Wishing Well. The image of eyes, black eyes winking from a gory red slit, hiding. My hands and feet are buzzing, vibrating, I feel like I'm going to be sick, but Marianne's still talking: "—tried to scare you off, but he was always there, he— And then Jouly, oh Jesus—"

"Where is Jouly?"

"I don't know," squeezing my hands so hard it hurts, really hurts, I can barely feel it. "I think he got her. I tried with her, too, but she doesn't get it, she's just a dumb little kid. Then I tried to hide her at Rainbows, but she went back. . . . The longer you stay, you know, the worse it gets." She touches her lips. "It'll never come off now."

My own lips are numb, numb like my hand, like my brain, as if I've just taken poison. Skull and crossbones, black and blood-red, that sweet quicksilver grace: *See? I*

told you she's an artist. What's mine is yours. I love you.
The sun is unbearably hot.

Then she drops her grip, gets back to her feet, her
shadow my shade. Balled tissue to her eyes, dirty white
clump and "I have to go," she says. She sounds incredibly
tired. "You should, too. Before he comes back."

"Wait," through the numbness, trying to think, think
faster than the pain already bearing down on me like a
wave, tidal wave so high I can't see the crest. "Where are
you going? Where—"

"Don't ask," but not mad anymore, no more Scaryanne: just Marianne, just a girl like me and "Bye, Maggy,"
she says, and hobbles off, grimy and haggard and scared
across the plaza, those awful spike-heeled boots, her feet
are probably bleeding by now. . . . My own feet hurt, a
dry swollen throb as I gather my stuff and start off in the
opposite direction, hurrying toward the bus stop, toward
home, every step an ache, every thought worse than the
last—

You're the one, Mags. I knew it right away.
Street girls, skwatters—they're dumb, right?
I never thought he'd go after you.

The bus is crowded with tourists and shoppers, the
driver's angry dog-voice sawing through the noise: "Step
back! Step back or I ain't going nowhere!" I find a sliver
of seat, one leg in the aisle, crammed beside two old
ladies, one of them drenched in some suffocating perfume,
gardenia and air freshener, and the other one's sniffling,

sniffling, sniffling till I feel like punching her in the face, I
feel like screaming at them both—

—but it's not them, or the noise, or the heat, or the
edge of my bag digging into my ribs, not the headache, the
hunger, the sleepless grit in my eyes that even tears can't
wash away, tears I try to cover with one hand, wiping,
wiping until "Here," at my elbow, the sniffling woman:
she's holding out a handful of fresh tissues, pink and soft,
the lotiony kind. "Want some?"

I take the tissues and she smiles, I try to smile, too, but
I can't, all I can do is try not to cry, try to hold it, the way
you hold something too heavy or too hot: it's going to fall,
spill so you have to hurry, I have to hurry, off the bus and
down the street, telling myself *one more block, just get
home* where I can let it go, let it fall and break if it has to,
a million burning pieces, my breaking heart—Cole. Oh
Cole.

Head down and shuffling like a refugee, bag dragging,
I don't look up, *just keep going* until "Mags," like a voice
in my head, a ghost voice and there he is, blue smile and
shiny new sunglasses, right here in front of my building,
like a granted secret wish—

—but I can't talk to him now, not one word, I can't
say anything so I try to step past him, to get away but he
stops me easily, stands in front so I can't move and
"Mags," he says again. "Where were you?"

Mags, oh don't call me that, oh God don't cry: not like
this, in the street with people passing, some girl hanging

out by the building door, who's she? A new girl? His new girl? Too-big coat hanging down past her knees, hair and face half covered by a dangling scarf, horrible blank eyes—

—Raggedy Ann in her hand

—Jouly? "*Jouly?*" oh God, that can't be her—but it is, a zombie Jouly, threadbare and mute, she looks at me like she never saw me before as "I'm talking to you," Cole sharp to me. "Where the hell were you? We went all over, looking—"

"What are you *doing?*" I say through a throat full of barbed wire, because I don't know how to say what I mean, *what are you, why why why*. "What happened to her? Jouly, what did he—"

"Don't talk to her," he says, to me? no, to Jouly, who just stands there like a puppet, a ventriloquist's dummy, I reach for her scarf but she pulls away, her mouth a straight blue line and "Don't," Cole says to me, still smiling; sleek silver sunglasses, I can't see his eyes. "Leave Jouly alone, she's fine. . . . Where've you been?" and when I don't answer he takes my hand, squeezes it hard and "You better tell me," still smiling. "I know you didn't come home last night. Your poor mother was really worried, you know."

My mother? "You talked to Monica?" jerking my hand away. "You went upstairs?"

And he laughs, like he's pulled off some great practical joke, a joke on me and "Sure I talked to her," he says, "we had a very nice chat." Hand in his pocket, cash in hand, he flashes it at me and "She's not too bright, though, is she? Oh well. Can't have everything—"

Her purse always open on the counter, trusting Monica, *he's darling* and "Give me that!" my cry but he laughs again, pushes me away, playfully, like you'd push a puppy—then harder, when I won't stop, when I come back again and "Cut it out," he says; he's not smiling anymore. "Let's go."

My heart is pounding, a hard and trembling beat, the tidal wave swamping my air but "I'm not going anywhere with you," I say. "Go away."

"Mags—"

"Stop calling me that! You're a liar, you lied to me, go *away*!"

He doesn't move, doesn't speak, just slides down the sunglasses and—looks at me, with those beautiful, beautiful eyes, those eyes I loved before I even knew him—

—and a part of me . . . *yearns* for him, a part of me, most of me wants to go to him, cry myself out on his shoulder, put myself in his hands

because he's so beautiful, because

I love you

—and he sees all this, I see him see it and his smile comes back, triumphant, unsurprised: a smile at me, but not about me because it's really all about him, Cole smiling at Cole and "Don't be stupid," he says, still smiling, "you know you belong to me. You're my little artist, right? You're going to do my portrait—"

"No," my whisper, my voice like broken glass. The wave descending. I can't hold it anymore, trembling, digging in my bag, I can barely see to find my keys—

—as "Come on," he says to Jouly, then to me "Tell your friend Marianne—" something, I can't hear, I slam the door on him—

—and the first thing I see, I almost trip over, is Paz: there in the pile of take-out flyers, newspaper huddle and "Paz!" as I scoop him up, hold him tight. "Oh my God, Paz, are you all right?"

Frantic and purring, rubbing his face on my hand, he seems OK, just scared—but then I see it, just between his shoulders: fur missing, a dark mark like a burn, a brand, a red-hot finger, "Oh Paz, what *happened*?" but he only purrs, rubs, so I carry him back upstairs, pausing in the stairwell to take a breath, like an air bubble underwater, the weight of the water pressing down, just a few more steps—

—into the stink of smoke, Monica hyper and babbling, lurching off the sofa, turning the TV down: "You're here! Oh Maggy, I was so *worried*— But then your boyfriend came, he told me you were fine—"

"He's not my boyfriend." I set Paz down; he heads immediately for his bowl. "What happened to Paz? Why'd you let him out?"

"I didn't, your—oh Maggy, what's the matter?" Peering at me, who knows what my face looks like. "Did you have a fight with your boyfriend? Did he—"

"Stop saying that! He's not my boyfriend! And don't ever let him in here again. You hear me? Not ever!"

"Maggy?" as I turn away, turn down the hall that stretches forever, I'll never be able to stop . . . but at last I reach it, my bedroom, my burrow where as soon as I slam the door it all comes pouring out, the wave breaks into sobs that drown me, shake me like a shipwreck tide, hurt so deep I can't touch the bottom—

—as the door opens again, Monica on the threshold, arms out as without a word she comes to me and holds me tight, holds me like she used to back when she was my mom—and I just cry, cry until I can't anymore, until she wipes my face with tissues and brings me an aspirin, a glass of lukewarm juice, pulls the shades and tucks me in and "Shhh," her hand on my forehead, "it's going to be all right, Maggy, you'll see. It's all going to be all right."

8

Sunset again. Shadows pressing on the shade, quiet TV drone, all the day lost to sleep, *lethe*, unconsciousness. And now I stir, under piled blankets, like an animal in its lair, a wounded animal waiting to see if it will live or die. My legs ache from walking, my eyes ache from crying. Everything hurts.

I open my sketchbook.

No pictures at first, nothing planned, I just let the pencil do what it wants and what it wants is all darkness: blacked-out windows, deserted rooms, long shadows that look like creeping vines, like claws. Beside me Paz lies curled and dozing, the burn a sullen red on his back, I put some ointment on it before. How did you get burned, Paz? One of Monica's cigarettes? Or was it someone else? I feed him Fishies, one by one, almost a whole bag of Fishies; my poor Paz. An innocent bystander. Monica, too.

Darkness rising past the windows, darkness on the page. Darkness in me, an arctic cold, dead and numb like my numb hand, the feeling still hasn't come back. Maybe that's better. It hurts to feel.

Now my pencil draws a backdrop landscape: downtown, the promenade, the skwatters, the Wishing Well: like ruins on fast-forward, *trapped stars*, like flies in amber. Fossils for a dead time. . . . Dead time, dead hand, dead love—as my pencil moves, grinds, hurricane lines, a force so fierce it makes holes in the paper, digs through to the other side, to *mags* in a circle, *I watched you drawing. I saw you every day* but that was just a lie, wasn't it, just a tool to use on me. A tool I let him use; why? *The losers, the lonely ones away from the herd, kissaholic* but I wasn't lonely that way, was I? I was just—alone. With my sketchbook. With my Z-ray vision. *No matter what else you do, keep drawing*, who said that? *He's, like, fuckin' weird . . . like in a movie or something*, who said *that*?

And the pencil keeps moving, drawing, drawing out of that darkness a figure, not quicksilver but black ice, Cole, the Cole I could never draw before: Cole in his parka,

Cole and his blue smile, still completely beautiful but *wrong*, wrong and distorted like a fun-house monster, hair twisting like seaweed, eyes a two-way mirror reflecting back on, what?—

—on *nothing*: real nothing, like absolute zero, a walking, talking black hole—

—and all around him, like a halo, the wild nimbus of hunger, mindless hunger, a blue mouth open and sucking—

—a mouth that I fed, didn't I, and kept on feeding: with my time, my body, my love, my art. With *me*. And for what?

My hand is shaking, burning; I feel sick, like eating spoiled food, rotten meat, like the smell from Marianne's sweater. But I don't stop, I keep going, keep drawing Cole with his arms spread wide, not to embrace but to capture, sweep off the streets, *they were never there when I needed them*, needed them for what, Cole? Sidekicks? sex toys? followers? food? When you're that empty you need to get *full*, right, but how can you fill yourself except by feeding, feeding off the girls, all the girls, Abby and Erika and Tasha, Kyla and Doucette, Jouly and Marianne.

And *mags*.

Where are you right now, Marianne? Hiding downtown, in one of the shelters? Or somewhere on a bus, riding, running away? Are you going back home, do you have a home? Where were you before you met Cole? . . . I never even asked her, did I? her or Jouly, poor Jouly. All I saw, could see, was him. *My little artist.* Except I didn't

see him at all.

But now I do.

Knock-knock, it's Monica, a little two-knuckle tap, she sticks her head around the door. Hand with the cigarette thoughtfully kept out of my room, gentle hospital-voice: "How are you feeling, honey?" She hasn't called me honey in a long time.

"I'm fine."

"Are you hungry? You didn't eat all day. . . . Should I fix some soup? Or Chinese, I could run out and get some Chinese—"

"No, that's OK."

Head to one side, her face a shadow backlit by hall light, what does she see when she looks at me? A girl crying over her boyfriend, a sentimental teenage broken heart? "School called," reluctantly. "Twice. A woman, Susan something, Susan Gallo?"

"Galliano." School, like a planet I once visited, a million light-years away. I can't think of school right now. "Don't worry about it. If she calls again I'll talk to her."

She hesitates. I know she wants to help, to do something so "Do me a favor?" I say, as Paz jumps down, nimble, tail up, has he forgotten what happened to him? What did happen? but I don't ask, maybe Monica saw and maybe she didn't and maybe she wouldn't remember if she did. "Feed Paz, OK? Half a can of Mister Whiskers. And fill his water bowl?"

"OK, honey," nodding, turning to go—then pausing, hand on the knob, like she wants to say something, do something, make it all better; but she can't. No one can. So she looks at me and I look at her, until "Thanks," I say, and softly she closes the door.

Now Paz sleeps in a blanket cocoon; Monica sleeps with the TV on low. I don't sleep. It's four a.m. I stand by the window, eating a handful of crackers, nacho-cheddar flavor, and drinking oolong tea from a juice glass; no clean mugs.

For a while it was raining, long gray free-fall needles, but now it's turned to mist swept by the wind, a wind that rattles the leftover leaves on the trees, old dry leaves, dead. Dead a long time ago, but still hanging on. But spring is coming, whether it feels like it or not.

I watch out the window; what do I expect to see? I don't know. I eat the crackers out of my good hand; I keep watching. From the living room I hear Monica snoring, like a friendly old slobbery dog. On the TV, people laugh, a muted and faraway sound.

I finish the crackers. My other hand, my drawing hand, aches; I've been working for hours, like a dam bursting, working on one drawing: my portrait of Cole. Black hole, black eyes, his face fills the page, fills it with emptiness; where does it come from, so much emptiness? Then I wrote the date, and *MAGGY* in caps underneath.

No more *mags* in a circle; no more Mags at all.

After that I cleaned out my bag. All kinds of junk, paper napkins, some quarters and nickels I stacked on my dresser, cracked pencils, candy wrappers, a drugstore receipt for Monica's Winstons. The PROMISE ME button. Slim silver tube of lipstick, Midnight Kiss, half used. I threw it all away.

The wind rises and fades. On the bed my sketchbook is open; I close the cover—with both hands, pressing, like what's inside might get out—then slide the book into my bag.

On the street below me, nothing. I keep watching. The tea is stale and cold.

Two more hours till dawn.

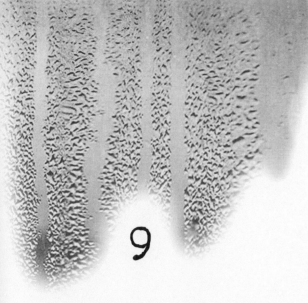

9

Morning sun a sparkle on the water of the Wishing Well,
furled buds on the tree branches like tiny hands clutched
tight against the chill, as a moving stream of office work-
ers, coffee-cart vendors, transit cops pass me shivering on
a bench, why did I come down here? I don't know. It's
early, too early, too late to sit with a jumbo cappuccino
and a raisin bagel; the bagel is like a rock, even the pigeons won't eat it. I blow on the cappuccino, feel the
steam against my lips—

—and then I see her, here where she shouldn't be,
hands in pockets, she sees me too and "Hey," approaching, shoulders tight, high-wire walk like if she stops she'll

fall. A coat instead of the sweater and jean jacket, sneak- ers instead of spiky boots: running shoes. Running-away shoes. But she didn't run away, did she, she perches beside me on the bench and "Why are you still here?" I say to Marianne.

She peers at me. "Why are you? —You look like shit, by the way. Are you OK?"

Am I OK, I can't begin to answer that so "I thought," I say, "that you were leaving."

"Leaving for where?"

"I don't know." I hand her the cappuccino, watch as she takes a slow sip: frown lines harsh around her lips, blue stain like a lingering bruise. "Just—away. Back home, or—"

"Home. Right." People hurry by, tote bags and brief- cases, high heels and phones, people from another world. She takes another sip, hands it back. "I was heading down to the bus terminal. But then I heard."

My heart gives an ugly bound. "Heard what?"

"About Jouly."

Jouly in the street, the Jouly I'd never seen before and "I saw her," I say. "She was with Cole, and she—"

"She's in the hospital now. Street Mike's," which means St. Mike's, Saint Michael's, the welfare hospital where the street people have to go. "Angela told me, you know Angela? So I went down there, to Emergency, but they wouldn't let me in to see her. Family only, they said. Like she even *has* a family."

"What happened?" past the noise of my heart, mind's-eye memory of a sidewalk puppet, *Leave Jouly alone, she's fine* and "They found her here," Marianne says. Squinting in the slant of sun, no, not squinting, crying. Squeezing her eyes against the tears, like you squeeze the edges of a cut to stop the bleeding. "Just lying there like a, a bag of garbage or something. She was, what do they call it? when you're out in the cold too long?"

I take her hand in mine. It's freezing. "Exposure."

"Exposure. Yeah. To Cole. —Oh Maggy," rough, "I tried to tell her, I tried to get her to see—"

"Is she going to be all right?" but even as I ask I know the answer, how could the Jouly I saw ever be all right? Dead eyes. Used up. Exposure—

"You talking about that girl?" A squeaky voice, pointy face stuck into mine: another girl, two girls, skwatter-girls. Thirteen maybe, way too much makeup, grimy gloves with the fingers cut out. Like Jouly wears. Used to wear. "You *know* her?" says Squeaky-Voice again. "The one they found *right here*?"

"I heard," avid Girl Number Two, "that she was, like, *dead*."

"She's not dead!" Marianne shouts, then looks away, looks down at her hands, clenched hands. "Get away from me. Go play in traffic."

"She goes around with that Cole guy," says Squeaky. Purple-red lipstick, so dark it looks black. Or blue. "I see him all the time. . . . He's really *hot*," and they giggle, they both giggle, they peer at me and "Hey," says Girl Number Two. "Don't you, aren't you like his—"

"No," I say. "I'm not. And you better stay away from him. He'll eat you like a snack, he'll—"

"Oh yeah right," Squeaky, hands on hips, like I'm, what? the jealous girlfriend, *stay away from my man*, if it wasn't so terrible I'd laugh. Or cry.

"Fresh meat," says Marianne grimly. "Go on, go home, if you have one."

"Yeah right bitch," and they scamper away, fast and wobbly on their heels, absorbed into the morning crowd and "Just like Jouly," Marianne says, wiping her eyes on her sleeve. "They don't listen, they only believe what they see."

The rhythmic splash of the Wishing Well, like an urging, murmuring voice; somewhere a siren rises, falls, rises again. I dig in my bag, pull out my book, flip it open on the bench, the portrait page and "Here," I say; my voice sounds far away. "Take a look."

Marianne flinches back, as if it's Cole himself glaring out at her; then she takes the book in her hands, holds it fiercely close. The sun rises higher. I unzip my coat, old winter coat; Cole's green jacket is in the Dumpster behind our building, tied tight in a garbage bag. My stomach aches.

Finally Marianne looks up, not at me but at the Wishing Well crowd, the straggling skwatter-girls and "They should see this," she says. Her eyes are hard and bright. "Everybody should! Then they'd know what he is—"

"What he isn't," I say.

She's still holding the book, like a shield now, close to her chest and "How did you do this? How did you get it so, so perfect?" and she turns it so we can both look, heads together over the page as "Let me see," from behind us, right behind us and I slam the book closed, snatch it back an instant before his hand, grabbing hand can reach, up on our feet and "Hello, girls," says Cole.

Sunglasses and shiny parka, that too-sweet smell like burning flowers and "Why can't I see?" through his smile, like a knife jabbed through a curtain. "It's about me, right?"

"Leave us alone," I say, book under one arm, gripping Marianne's hand in mine. I can feel her shaking. I can feel myself shaking. "I told you before, go away."

He sits on the bench where we were sitting, tilts his head toward the sun; it glares off his glasses, blind eyes and "Calm down, Mags," still smiling; which is worse, the name or the smile? "I don't mind if you draw me. I *wanted* you to draw me."

"I don't care what you want. I—"

"Jouly," says Marianne. She squeezes my hand, a cold spasmodic squeeze, to, what? make herself brave? Scary-anne, getting courage from *me*? and "Jouly," she says again, louder, to Cole. "What happened? What did you do to her?"

But he doesn't answer, doesn't even look at her: only at me, blank silver stare and "I came to visit you," he says. "But you weren't home."

Home. Paz. Monica. I take a step forward; Marianne shrinks back. "Stay away from my house." My voice is tinny, weak, I try to make it stronger. "Stay *away* from my—"

"But I wanted a nice cup of vodka tea." Grinning. White teeth bright against the blue. The hunger comes off him in waves, like cold from a freezer, a freezer buried in the ground. A grave. "I wanted to *be* with you, Mags. . . . And where the fuck were you?" turning on Marianne who just—dwindles, shrivels up in his gaze like paper in a fire. "At a shelter or someplace? picking out a nice new coat? You look like a bag lady, you know that? Like shit swept up off the street. . . . So where were you, bag lady?"

"Jouly," she says, but he doesn't hear, or hearing, doesn't care, isn't listening anyway and "Stupid bitch," he says, sighs, like she's a job he has to finish. "You come with me now."

And she actually takes a step, trembling all over, like a dog creeping forward to be punished, like she can't say no—but I can, I'm still holding her hand, holding it tight and "Go away," I say to him. My voice shakes, but I won't let go. "Leave us alone."

"Oh Mags," through that smile, "don't be stupid. Don't tell me what to do. Don't *ever*—"

—and he's fast, oh God he's fast, quicksilver but I knew it was coming, that snatching hand, I yank her back hard and "Run!" my cry, out loud? in my head? "Marianne *run*—"

—through the crowd, our hands locked together, sketchbook tight under my arm, run where? I don't know but we go, sidestep and dash, obstacle course of the crowd around us, dart around the benches, jump past the curb—

—but wherever we go, however we run, he's there already: beside a coffee cart, behind an idling cab, leaping down from a red brick half-wall, hands out and grinning, *Gotcha!* like it's a game, like it's fun, maybe it is fun for him. Marianne's panting, big sucking gasps, clutching me like she's drowning, hanging on me like I can save her, like I know where we're going but I don't, I'm just running, I can't melt us through the crowd like he does but while we stay in the center, in the moving throng, he can only follow, he can't take us down—

into the dark the hunger like falling into someone's mouth

no

—but I can't keep this up, this flat-out run and dodge: already my lungs feel like cement, my sketchbook digs hard into my arm so "Come on!" as I haul Marianne sideways, bulling through the crowd like fording a river—people shoving back, "Hey!" and "Watch it!"—as "Oh God," Marianne pants, "oh God oh God," because now he's running *beside* us, right beside us like jogging in place—and laughing, to show it *is* just a game to him, a cruel game he can stop anytime he wants, grab us when he wants

like now

"—oh *God*—"

NO

"Here!" as I hit the door, really hit it, and momentum flings us hard inside: to miss the milling counter line by inches then crash into an empty table, send it slewing, *clang!* the flying napkin dispenser, gritty sugar spill, "Aw shit!" as a woman leaps up, leaking brown pool on her skirt and "Hey!" hard behind us, a guy's voice: not Cole's. Casey's. "What the *hell* do you—Maggy?" Hands on my arms, eyes wide. He got another haircut. Marianne is hunched against the counter, weeping, or choking, a hard coughing sound. "Maggy! What's wrong?"

"Nothing," my gasp, I can barely speak. Cole is outside, on the sidewalk; I see him through the window, the Blue Mirror window, an angry moving blur. "Can we—just rest—for a minute?"

He looks at me—only a second, but it lasts a long time—then "In there," pointing behind him: EMPLOYEES ONLY, a haphazard pile of coats, plastic-cup towers, stacked bales of paper towels where we drop, half falling; I'm still gripping my sketchbook, my fingers don't want to unclench. Marianne heaves, trying not to throw up, head hung between her knees and "Just breathe," I say. My arms and legs are trembling. Everything smells like coffee. "Just breathe, you'll be OK."

Just breathe. In. Then out. Then in again. I lean back against a paper-towel bale, waiting for my heart to slow down; I think of Cole outside, waiting, ready for the next move in the game and "Now what?" says Marianne when she can talk, hands on either side of her head as if she doesn't hold it, it might fall off. Her eyes are wide, cheeks spotted red, two bright spots like a doll's. Like Raggedy Ann's. "That fuckhead's still out there."

"I know."

"He won't go away, he won't leave us alone, he never—"

"I know."

"What are we going to *do*?"

I shake my head, hand still on my sketchbook, sweat-damp and warped from the force of my grip. My heart is still pounding. My head is still pounding. I squeeze out some napkins from the bale, some for her, some for me, wet them at the little corner sink, warm-water trickle and we wipe our faces, Marianne wipes her eyes because she's crying, silent tears, she looks—defeated. She looks like Jouly, lost and scared. Am I like that, too?

"Maggy? What're you doing?"

Am I? I want to know. I *need* to know. Otherwise it'll always hurt. Otherwise he'll keep coming back. Black eyes peering out of red meat, black hole disguised as a human being—

—and Marianne half off the bale, "What are you *doing*? You're not going outside, are you? Jesus, Maggy, don't! He's still out there, he'll see—"

—but I want him to see, I have to see, so I walk out of the storeroom, past the line of customers, past where

Casey's kneeling to clean up the sugar mess, straight up to the window, my window, the Maggy Klass Memorial Booth, where I stand with my hand on the glass, numb hand, right hand, drawing hand—

—and just like that, like bad magic he's there, palm pressed to mine, staring in through Blue Mirror glass, "Blue Mirror" glass, and he's saying something, I can't hear, I don't need to: all I have to do is look at him, all of him, his tall, lean grace, his eyes, the endless hunger of that wet blue mouth

I love you

which is the terrible thing, the worst of all: not because it's true—it's not, he doesn't love me, love's not possible for him—but because it's all he has, that reflex, nothing real left inside at all. Maybe he was real once, but now he's only . . . bait. For the hunger. Bait, twisting on the hook, his face twisting now as I lift my sketchbook, my drawing, pressing it up against the window, the Blue Mirror his mirror, staring in at his own face

look Cole see your little artist made the portrait this is who you are what you are all you are

and he sees

and jerks back, really *jerks*, like he just got a shock, a burn, hand snatched away from the glass, eyes wide

then rears back and spits at the window, at my face right behind it, tears on my cheeks and "That's it," Casey beside me, voice tight, clenching the cleaning rag. The spit slides down, an ugly, cloudy lump. "I'm calling security, I'm not going to put up with this shit—"

—but "No," I say; I put my hand on his arm. "Don't, it's OK, he's going away," and while I'm saying it he does, backing from the mess on the window, back from his face in the glass, back into the swirl of the street and like magic, quicksilver

Make a wish, Mags

he's gone.

"But what if he's still out there?" Marianne says for the twentieth time, even though I know for sure that it's all right, we can walk to the Wishing Well, the bus stop, go anywhere we feel like now, I don't know how I know this but I do.

"Marianne, stop, OK? Trust me, it's all right."

"On my lunch," says Casey, speed-wrapping sandwiches, "I'll drive you guys home."

"Casey, really, it's all right. He's not going to—"

"Let me," he says; he puts his hand on my shoulder, gives a gentle squeeze. "OK? Just let me do this for you."

His trusty Toyota is parked down the block; as we walk there, he's scanning the street, checking out the crowd: looking for trouble, for Cole. Marianne keeps looking, too, head turning like a nervous tic; when we get to the car she makes me climb in the backseat with her, as if we're little kids.

I could keep telling them both not to worry, but I'm too tired, so tired I could sleep for a week, so tired I barely listen as they talk: *Where should I take you* and *Staying at Maggy's*, not that far but it seems to take forever to drive there. Head against the window, I can feel all the bumps in the road but it's pleasant somehow, peaceful, like being on a kiddie ride, one of those little trains at the amusement park that go around and around. Casey turns on the radio, the classical station; Marianne changes the station; Casey changes it back.

When we get there he sits watching, idling outside, to see us safely inside, Marianne following as I trudge up the stairs, down the hall, digging out my keys and "Does your mother care," asks Marianne, "if I, like, sleep here? For a couple of days?"

"My mother," I say, around a yawn, a huge, jaw-creaking yawn; I can barely keep my eyes open. "My mother wouldn't care if you moved in. She—" as I turn the key, Monica's voice, "Here she is now!" half relieved, half freaked out, oh now what? as we step in, scarecrow Marianne and me looking like a tumbleweed: to see Monica on the sofa, hands-folded tense beside some woman, official-looking woman in a brown print suit, briefcase open on the floor, papers scattered on the coffee table and "Maggy," says Monica, all brittle and bright, "this is Mrs. Galliano. Susan Galliano? From school?"

10

Pfft, Marianne blows her straw paper at me, then reaches to pick it up and tuck it neatly into the trash. White apron askew, too-tight black golf shirt, hair sort of pulled back in a bun; she has a ton of hair, when it's clean. "Move over," she says, handing me my cappuccino, setting down her own Coke. The Blue Mirror's not crowded—late spring sunshine's got everyone outside, walking, skating, soaking up the warmth—so it's just us, and some old guy reading the newspaper. "Let's see what you're working on."

"Just some stuff," I say, as she inspects the pages, sketchbook pages filled with faces: lots of little mini-portraits from the streets, from school, from Monica's clinic—I went with her, she asked me to and I did. Afterward we went out for Chinese. . . . I shouldn't really be drawing now, I suppose, I should be doing homework, or at least trying to make a bigger dent in it, all the ton still stuffed in my bag.

I have to admit, I haven't gotten all the way back into school. I mean, I'm going to classes now, way more than I did before, almost every day. But it all seems even more pointless, after everything I've been through. Except for Drawing II.

I guess I should be glad they took me back; I owe Ms. Onwiski for that. She took my side at the reinstatement thing, passing around my sketchbook—*You have to understand, Maggy's an artist, a budding artist gathering her material*—which did a lot to convince them that I was more than just another truant, just a skwatter out running the streets. Although in a weird way it was Monica who helped most of all, by being a weepy vodka mess at the meeting, or hearing, or whatever it was. At least they saw I wasn't lying about having to help out at home.

The thing is, though, I fell so far behind, I might have to repeat the grade anyway, it'd be so much easier just to quit altogether but Marianne keeps saying *Don't you dare do what I did, stay in school, dumbass.* And Casey says *For once, she's right.* He always talks like that to her face. Behind her back he says *Marianne's OK. She can't work half the machines, you know, and she has no clue how to talk to customers. But she's really trying.*

Trying, yeah. She's still staying at my house, waiting to get into the transitional housing thing at Rainbows. It's kind of a pain, sharing my space, but kind of fun, too; sort of like having a sister. A feral sister. The only really bad part is she snores like a dog. Like Monica. Worse than Monica. Maybe it's because she's warm for a change, warm all the way through; maybe it's because she's safe and she knows it and can finally relax. *It's so nice to sleep inside*, remember?

Plus she's in love with Paz, she's always playing with him and bringing him stuff from work, little treats, scraping the lettuce off the day-old ham and cheeses: *He likes it, OK? Especially the Havarti cheese, the cat is like a freak for Havarti.* Paz's fur is all grown in, now, around the burned place on his back, even though he'll always have a scar there, bumpy and pinkish-white. But a scar means you healed, right? It proves that you survived.

Now Marianne taps the page: "Oooh, I like this one," like she's ordering from a catalog. Tall guy with dreadlocks, loose jacket, and tight pants, "Didn't get his number or anything, did you? How about a name? God, you're totally useless. . . . I saw your friend yesterday, did I tell you?"

"Don't call him that." I see him sometimes, too; I wish I didn't, but I do. Not doing much of anything, just ghosting around by the Wishing Well, sometimes talking to girls. I never like to look at him for long.

Marianne slurps crushed ice up the straw, blows it noisy back into her glass. "I'll tell you, he looks like total shit nowadays, all sucked-in and skinny and— Now what's that face about? Girl, you better not be feeling *sorry* for—"

"I'm not," which is true, I don't feel sorry for Cole, how could I? But I do feel something for him, or about him: an ache inside, a hard, small sorrow, like seeing something that you thought was good turn into something horrible . . . is that regret? Or pity? I don't know. I do know he won't look at me, if our paths cross by mistake. He just hurries by, like he doesn't even know who I am.

"You still have his picture?" she says, tapping my book; she means the portrait of Cole. I nod. I don't like to look at that, either; I have it paper clipped to the pages before and after, so I don't open on it by mistake. Marianne's asked me fifty times how I knew it would "work" on him, like it was some move I had planned; I've given up telling her I don't know. How could I have known? I just—did it.

Yet even at the last, there at the window, he was still so . . . beautiful. I know how that sounds, but it's true.

"I still say you should put it up somewhere," she says. "Like one of those criminal posters, right?" displayed, like a warning to the girls, all the skwatter-girls who need to see what he is, to know. *"Wanted: For fucking over Jouly."*

The name makes us both quiet. Jouly. We called again and again, but they never would let us talk to her, they wouldn't even tell us if she was still in there or not. Was it really "exposure," or something even worse? *He really hurt her, they had to send her to a hospital upstate.*

Will we see her again? Will anyone? I don't know. I saved my drawings of her, happy-faced chipmunk, loopy blue smile; it hurts to look at them, but it's a way of keeping her with us, keeping her alive.

Casey keeps talking about showing my stuff, too, not just the drawing of Cole but all of it, all the stuff in my sketchbook, take it to a gallery or something, or maybe put it up here, have a show in the Blue Mirror. He was the one who called the guy from the newspaper: TEEN ARTIST DRAWS ATTENTION TO THE HOMELESS, it was only a tiny little article, but it helped at that hearing. Now Monica has it stuck up on the refrigerator.

"Do it for Jouly," Marianne says now, nudging me. For Jouly, for Marianne; for me? Maybe. "Do it for—"

"Do what?" as Casey comes up beside us, smiles at me, raises his eyebrows at Marianne and "How come you're not working?" he says, pretending to be annoyed. "Trainees don't deserve breaks, do they?"

"I am working." She sticks out her tongue at him. Her lips are almost pink again. "I'm trying to get this deadbeat

customer to buy something. Or at least do her homework," as she slides out of the booth and he slides in,
biscotti in a napkin and "Here, try this," he says. "It's
almond-fudge. . . . Not slacking off, are you, M?" He calls
me "M" now. "I'm keeping my eye on you, you know."

"I know."

We sit there quiet for a minute, just looking at each
other, him smiling that smile he seems to keep just for me.
I'm not sure exactly what it means: he's never asked me
out or anything, or even really flirted with me, although
You're an idiot, Marianne keeps telling me, *he's crazy
about you. Anybody can see that.*

*He is not. Anyway he's like twenty-two, he doesn't
want someone in high school.*

You are an idiot.

Now she's back behind the counter, struggling with
the espresso machine, thin white geyser of steam and
"Damn it!" she wails, leaping backward. "Casey! Help!"

"Just turn the—no, the other one. The *other* one—"
as he scoots out of the booth, as Marianne swears, as I
turn back to my book, my almost-done page: nothing special, just another Blue Mirror street scene, past and present jumbled up together. Afternoon crowds like flocks of
summer birds, surging over the promenade; a hard-hat
ballet dancer, a giant walking briefcase, two cell phones
yelling face-to-face. By the Wishing Well a group of girls,
a herd of soiled gazelles; behind them, half-hidden, stands
a pale Raggedy Ann, hands clasped in front of her, her

eyes sewn shut. Marianne's there, too, pink lips and wild hair, her face in a furious knot; behind her Casey sits like Buddha, head shorn and smiling, in a giant heart-shaped cup. In the background, in a building like the little crooked house, Monica lies inert on the sofa, becoming the sofa, its worn-out plaid pattern her skin, as behind her, atop her, prowls Paz the Panther, his tail an exclamation point. Far away, on the dark rim of the horizon, so far it's almost off the page, is a tiny dark smear: is it Cole? Or just a memory of him?

See? I told you she's an artist.

And at the very bottom, right above where my signature goes, there's someone else, someone new, someone I've never drawn before. A tall girl with a battered messenger bag, hair in a knot, half-smile—is it?—on her face: MAGGY-M-Maggy, bent over her sketchbook, drawing with her long pencil-fingers a blue-mirrored map of the world.

She looks good.